T0304348

Reantasy, Montreal

The book to read, the place to be

A Fictional Biography

DAVID MAKIN

authorHOUSE®

AuthorHouse™
1663 Liberty Drive
Bloomington, IN 47403
www.authorhouse.com
Phone: 1 (800) 839-8640

Published by AuthorHouse   10/05/2015

ISBN: 978-1-5049-5072-5 (sc)
ISBN: 978-1-5049-5071-8 (e)

Library of Congress Control Number: 2015915208

Dedication

To my late mother Shirley and for Sharron

Foreword

I have known David Makin the author of *Reantasy, Montreal*
for a couple of years. We are Anglophones (English speaking
Quebecers) both Montreal born and raised.

Although we are both bilingual (able to speak French and English)
we will always be addressed or be termed as Anglos.

Montreal is a unique city unlike any other city I have seen or
visited. Montreal is truly a multi-cultural, cosmopolitan city and at
one time the biggest and richest city in Canada.

David is soft-spoken, well-groomed with an open and inviting
personality, a truly dashing individual. David also has a vast
knowledge of just about everything, and he takes it upon himself to
share and research subjects that interest him.

I knew that David was writing a manuscript and when I questioned
him about it, he calmly explained to me the concept behind
Reantasy, Montreal I was immediately intrigued.

Imagine my surprise when he asked if I would like to read a few
pages, a chapter or (what he likes to term) an 'episode' from his
book *Reantasy, Montreal.* I was at once both taken aback and

honoured by the request. He also asked me to relay my honest
feedback to him.

Later that same day David emailed me a few rough pages from a
chapter and an 'episode' he had written, I could not wait to read it.

Just a reminder, that David and I were born and raised in Montreal,
and for me it was as if I was transported back in time to my childhood.
The references of people, places and events and his attention to detail
are quite remarkable. The trivia of Canadian, Quebec and Montreal
connections are very interesting and fun to read.

The amount of time he spent researching certain events for his
book must be staggering. But in the end, the effort put in pays off
in spades.

Reantasy, Montreal intertwines aspects of a reality with a fictional
or a fantasy life. *Reantasy* is the only word that best describes the
story within the book.

David's writing style is quite different than what I am used to. He
is able to write in different styles and demonstrates many different
styles though out *Reantasy, Montreal.*

Reantasy, Montreal is formatted in a way I have not seen in book
form. The recollections, events, brief histories & trivia throughout
the book are fun, personal and interesting.

The emoticons and symbols add a modern touch to an instant
classic. The background information supplied in each chapter of
Reantasy, Montreal informs the reader and does not distract from

the storytelling. The odd word he 'makes-up' along the way does not distract either.

Reantasy, Montreal starts off a little slow but soon 'grabs you' and holds your interest until the very end.

The chapter and 'episode' I read are well constructed, well written and highly entertaining. The 'episode' I read left me in stitches and I couldn't stop laughing to myself.

Reantasy, Montreal reads as though David is sitting at a table telling you a story.

Reantasy, Montreal is a walk back through time, for better or worse, good or bad, turmoil and triumphs, laughter and sorrow. Personally I cannot wait for *Reantasy, Montreal* to be released to the general public.

In writing this foreword, I am eagerly awaiting to see *Reantasy, Montreal* on the shelves of my local bookstore. What a treat that will be!

I will definitely be purchasing a few copies of *Reantasy, Montreal* not only for myself but for my friends and family as well!

Reantasy, Montreal is the book to read, the place to be.

Mark Mast
Montreal, 2015

Preface

People have always said to me that I am a great storyteller and that I should put the stories on paper. I have always thought about writing a book. Some have suggested I write an autobiography, others suggested a work of fiction would be better. One morning I awoke, sat at my desk, turned on my computer and began to write.

With no thought pattern, a story slowly began to develop, a story about a life born in Montreal, influenced by Quebec and Canadian events, scandals, controversies and politics, a life proud of Montreal's heritage, Quebec and Canadian culture and talent.

Within a few pages I realized I was writing a biography, a few pages later I thought to myself perhaps I was writing a work of fiction. Then I fully realized that I was adding some minor aspects of reality to a fantasy or fictional life I was making up as I went along. A reantasy of sorts!

Reantasy is a word or term that comes to mind when I combine an aspect of reality with a made up fantasy…thus the title of the book.

This fictional biography or reantasy novel remembers, reminds and recounts various recollections, events, brief histories & trivia as seen through the eyes and told by a fictional life lived mostly during the mid to late nineteen seventies in the city of Montreal.

During the nineteen-sixties the city of Montreal experienced an incredible economic boom.

With the growth of massive construction projects which included the Montreal Metro System and the city's hosting of Expo '67, put the city of Montreal on the 'map' and brought the city international status.

Economic growth for the city of Montreal continued with the construction of the Montreal-Mirabel International Airport (at one time the largest airport in the world), the extension of the Montreal Metro System, and the building of the Olympic Stadium for Montreal's hosting of the 1976 Summer Olympics.

Reantasy, Montreal is a fictional story of innocence, personal and sexual growth and a passage from childhood to adulthood during a fondly remembered bygone Montreal era.

David Makin
Montreal, 2015

chapter one

1962, now that was a year!

Some notable news events from around the world happened during 1962.

In the United Kingdom, The Sunday Times is the first newspaper to print a color supplement, while in France; French President Charles de Gaulle calls for and accepts Algerian independence. Uganda, Jamaica, Trinidad and Tobago also became independent.

Drummer Pete Best was replaced by Ringo Starr (a left-handed drummer playing a right- handed drum kit) who along with fellow band mates John Lennon, Paul McCartney and George Harrison known in the United Kingdom as The Beatles, released their first single Love Me Do.

During a 12 day stand-off (known as the Cuban Missile Crisis) between the United States and the Soviet Union, President Kennedy announces to the nation the existence of Soviet missiles in Cuba. Johnny Carson becomes the permanent host of The Tonight Show.

Premiering in UK theaters is the film Dr. No, starring Scottish actor Sean Connery portraying a fictional character named James Bond.

Meanwhile in Canada, The Trans-Canada Highway is opened. A Federal Election results in Prime Minister John Diefenbaker's Progressive Conservative Party reduced to a minority government.

In Montreal, (a city in the province of Québec) anticipates the opening of the forty-seven storey office tower, known as Place Ville Marie.

Also in Montreal, a married thirty-two year old mother of two, labors for sixteen hours and finally gives birth to her third child. Born two months premature, and placed in an incubator for six weeks, this adorable brown haired and brown eyed baby boy is soon released from the care of St. Mary's Hospital.

Upon arriving at his new home, the beautiful baby boy is hailed (by some) with awe and amazement while (with others) he is greeted with an array of confused emotions and mixed reviews.

Recollections, events, brief histories & trivia:

☹☹ One of my earliest recollections is as a baby being held up in the air, by a pair of strong arms and then seemingly falling to the floor.

Whether this actually happened is opened to discussion but it would explain the reason why to this day, I am afraid of heights.

👆☺ I recall grocery shopping with my mother at *Steinberg Grocery Stores*.

Founded in 1917, *Steinberg Grocery Stores* was at one time Quebec's largest supermarket chain.

By the early nineteen nineties the company would file for bankruptcy and the supermarket chain would be sold off to competitors *Metro, IGA* and *Provigo.*

👍☺ I would accompany my mother and older brother George, to the neighbourhood outdoor newsstand.

The newsstand was a 10 foot long by 5 feet wide by 6 foot high wooden square structure that would open for daytime business and be boarded down and locked at night.

The owner had quite the inventory of newspapers (from all over the world), a wide selection of magazines, pocketbooks, digests and comic books. My mother would let us both choose a comic book each.

My brother George would almost always choose a super-hero comic, while I would always choose a comic book from Western's Gold Key brand. It was the cover art of the comic books that awed me the most. I loved visiting the outdoor newsstand.

👍☺ Playing street hockey with the neighbourhood kids, chasing and watching many a rubber ball (also known as a bouncy ball) roll down into a street sewer.

✂☺ I recall my very first haircut at the neighbourhood barber shop.

My introduction to a barber shop (and a haircut) was when my mother instructed the barber to "Shave everything off…"

I had no idea what a ('bean shave' a style of a) buzz cut was until the barber, with electric clippers in hand began 'clipping' my hair off.

Seemingly my head would be a front lawn, my hair would be the green grass and the electric clippers were the lawnmower. 'Zoom, zoom' roared the electric clipper as it roamed upwards and downwards across my head.

Through the years I have worn my hair at different lengths and worn different hairstyles. As I have matured and grown older, I prefer the buzz cut. It is a short, low maintenance hairstyle.

👍☺ Play fighting with my older brother George, and then arguing with Ellen, my older sister.

👍☺ At home and at school I would speak English, while with my neighbourhood friends I would speak French. I was bilingual and did not know it.

🍴☺ I loved eating spaghetti with meat sauce. My mother's recipe for preparing a meat sauce was the best.

👍 ☺ Watching puppets Jerome the Giraffe and Rusty the Rooster, interact with Bob Homme on the CBC children's television show *The Friendly Giant* (1958-1985).

☺☹ Attempting to build a snowman during the cold winter months.

👍☺ My first passenger ride on a city bus, the clean shaven, and uniformed driver would sell bus tickets, supply and return change to boarding passengers from a change dispenser.

👍❄☺ I attended Expo 67 with my family.

My mother brought us kids to Expo 67. We visited the world's fair on Saint Helen's Island (Ile Sainte-Hélène) by way of the underground Montreal Metro System (Métro de Montréal).

Replacing many overloaded bus routes the underground Montreal Metro (an electricity powered transit train) opened to the public in October 1966.

The Montreal Metro originally consisted of 26 stations over three separate lines. We exited the metro at the Ile Sainte-Hélène station. It was my first time riding as a passenger; I thought it was so much fun!

The site of Expo 67 was overflowing with people and I was awestruck by the many pavilions and the crowds of people.

During his incumbency as mayor, Jean Drapeau (1916-1999) was responsible for securing the construction of Montreal Metro, Expo 67, and for securing the 1976 Montreal Summer Olympics.

The 1967 International and Universal Exposition were held in Montreal from April to October 1967. With the participation of 62 nations, Expo 67 was Canada's main celebration during its centennial year.

The official theme song for Expo 67 'Un jour, Un Jour' (Hey Friend, Say Friend) (1967) written by Stephane Venne with English lyrics by Marcel Stellman was recorded in both official languages. The song was selected from an international competition of 35 countries and 2220 entries.

'Un Jour, Un Jour' (Hey Friend, Say Friend) was criticized at the time for not containing or mentioning Montreal in its lyrics. Popular Quebec singers Michelle Richard and Donald Lautrec both recorded an English and French version of the song.

A few months before the official opening of Expo 67, Pierre Lalonde released the single 'We'll Have a Ball in Montreal' (Quand Tu Viendras a Montréal) in both official languages. Although not an official Expo 67 theme song, many Montrealers thought and believed that it was. 'We'll Have a Ball in Montreal' is a song that is fondly remembered.

Some location filming for the pilot episode of the ABC series *It Takes a Thief* (1968-1970), titled 'A Thief is a Thief is a Thief' was filmed at Expo 67. Robert Wagner starred as Alexander Mundy, a thief who in return for his release from prison works for the U.S. government.

*****

Once the world's fair ended, the site and pavilions continued as an exhibition called Man and His World (1968-1984) (French: Terre Des Hommes).

The exposition struggled for many years and as attendance declined, the condition of the site deteriorated and was eventually dismantled.

In 1976, a fire destroyed the outer skin of the dome of the Buckminster Fuller designed Montreal Biosphere (formerly the American Pavilion).

With the site falling in despair, the site began to resemble ruins of a futuristic city.

Buck Rogers in the 25ᵗʰ Century (1979-1981) used footage of Expo'67 to represent futuristic buildings.in the show. *Buck Rogers in the 25ᵗʰ Century* was a science fiction adventure television series (based on the character created by Phillip Francis Nolan) that aired on the NBC Television Network and starred Gil Gerard and Erin Gray.

Some location scenes of the two-part science fiction television series *Battlestar Galactica* (1978-1979) episode 'Greetings from Earth' were filmed at the ageing site of Man and his World *Battlestar Galactica*, aired on the ABC Television Network and starred Canadian actor Lorne Greene, Richard Hatch and Dirk Benedict.

*****

Lorne Greene (1915-1987) was born in Ottawa, Ontario and was a radio broadcaster for the Canadian Broadcasting Corporation earning the nickname "The Voice of Canada".

He starred as Ben Cartwright on the long running NBC television western series *Bonanza* (1959-1973). Lorne Greene recorded a number of country/western albums that he performed in a mixture of spoken word and singing, including the spoken word ballad 'Ringo' (1964).

He played private detective Wade Griffin on the short lived ABC series *Griff* (1973-1974) co-starring Ben Murphy.

Lorne Greene was also the voice and narrator of many documentaries including the nature series *Last of the Wild* (1974-1975) and the highly acclaimed nature series *Lorne Greene's New Wilderness* (1982-1987). Both of these nature series were produced by and broadcast on the CTV Television Network.

Lorne Greene also starred as Commander Adama on the *Battlestar Galactica* (1978-1979) spin-off series *Galactica 1980* (1980).

Lorne Greene passed away in 1987.

*****

To commemorate Montreal mayor Jean Drapeau, the site of Expo '67 was renamed Parc Jean Drapeau (1999) and the Ile Sainte-Hélène metro station (1967-2000) was also renamed Jean Drapeau (2000).

👍☺ I also enjoyed watching puppets Casey and Finnegan with Ernie Coombs (and his Tickle Trunk) on the CBC's children's show *Mr. Dressup* (1967-1996).

☹☹ My first day of elementary school (1968-1969) my mother accompanied me to school and showed me the bus route, which bus to take, which bus stop to get on and get off at.

I recall feeling panicked when my mother left me at school that first day.

☹☹ I recall being told to stop crying by my first grade teacher Miss Baker.

👍☺ Watching Saturday morning cartoons advertised as In Colour on a black and white television set.

👍☺ I enjoyed watching reruns of Ted Zeigler as *Johnny Jellybean* (1962-1963) a children's comedy show that aired on CFCF 12.

Ted Zeigler was an American writer and comedian, who starred as *Johnny Jellybean* (1962-1963) a children's comedy show produced in Montreal.

Ted Zeigler would also star in another Montreal produced children's show *The Buddies* (1967-1968) which co-starred Montreal born Peter Cullen.

Ted also appeared as a series regular on *The Sonny and Cher Comedy Hour* (1971-1974) and *The Hudson Brothers Razzle Dazzle Show* (1974-1975), which was produced in Toronto and aired on the CTV Television Network.

Ted Zeigler also starred in a popular series of television ads by Bell Canada for the Nellerphone, a fictional, incompetent rival telephone company competing for customers.

Ted Zeigler passed away in 1999.

Peter Cullen was born and raised in Montreal and co-starred with Ted Zeigler in the CFCF-12 produced children's show *The Buddies* (1967-1968).

Peter Cullen appeared in sketch comedy skits for the half-hour CBC produced series *Comedy Café* (1970) and *Zut!* (1970), both series were filmed in Montreal and aired on CBMT Channel 6.

Peter Cullen also appeared regularly on the music variety series *The Sonny and Cher Comedy Hour* (1971-1974) which was produced by the CBS Television Network. *The Hudson Brothers Razzle Dazzle Show* (1974-1975) a half-hour children's music variety show, starring brothers Bill, Mark, and Brett Hudson. Peter Cullen was also a regular on the CBC produced *The Wolfman Jack Show* (1976-1977).

Peter Cullen is probably best known for his body of work as a voice actor. His voice work includes *Dungeons & Dragons* (1983-1985), *The Transformers* (1984-1987), *The Transformers: Prime* (2010-2013).

👆☺ Watching the *Archie Show* (1968-1969) Based on the Archie comic book created by Bob Montana, the *Archie Show* was a 17 episode cartoon that incorporated music into the storyline.

The fictional group *The Archies* released a couple of record albums and the singles 'Sugar, Sugar' (1969) and 'Jingle Jangle' (1969), which were both written by Montreal born Andy Kim and Jeff Barry.

Andy Kim is a singer/songwriter born in Montreal, Quebec. He would move to New York to pursue a career in music.

Andy Kim released the album *How'd We Ever Get This Way* (1968) and the singles 'Shoot 'Em Up Baby' and 'How'd We Ever Get This Way', he co-wrote with Jeff Barry for the animated series The Archie Show (1968-1969), the hits 'Sugar, Sugar' and 'Jingle Jangle'.

The single 'Baby, I Love You' (1969) and a cover of The Ronettes 'Be My Baby' (1970) were huge chart hits in Canada.

In 1973, Andy Kim starred as rock star Rick Michaels, (who accidently falls into an empty swimming pool and is believed to have died) in the first season episode 'Sing a Song of Murder' on the CBS Television series *Barnaby Jones* (1973-1980) starring Buddy Ebsen and Lee Meriwether.

Andy Kim would release the mega international hit 'Rock Me Gently' (1974) and 'Fire Baby, I'm On Fire' (1974).

In 1980, Andy Kim would reinvent himself as Baron Longfellow and release the hits 'Amour' (1980) sung partially in English and French was a huge hit in the province of Quebec and 'I'm Gonna Need A Miracle Tonight' (1984).

In 2004, the song 'Did I Forget to Mention' was released and received considerable airplay on Montreal radio stations.

👍☺ I enjoyed watching reruns of *The Mighty Hercules* (1963-1966) and the Canadian animated television series *Rocket Robin Hood* (1966-1969).

Legendary Montreal radio and television personality Jimmy Tapp supplied the voice of the Hercules character.

👍☺ Playing with a yo-yo my mother bought me.

I would play with and practice the yo-yo every day. Practicing tricks with the yo-yo was the perfect past time and I brought the yo-yo with me everywhere, to school, running errands with my mother, riding on the bus.

The yo-yo and I were inseparable. My neighbours and classmates would whisper among themselves, when they would see me practicing yo-yo tricks, "There's goes David playing with his yo-yo!"

But I digress.

👍☺👍 Watching Montreal born William Shatner as Captain Kirk on the science fiction television series Star Trek.

Star Trek (1966-1969) was a science fiction adventure series created by Gene Roddenberry that I have always enjoyed. Star Trek was broadcast on the NBC Television Network and aired on the CTV Television Network.

Little did anyone know that *Star Trek* would spawn a number of novels, comics, video games and the spin-off television series; *The Animated Series* (1973-1974), *The Next Generation* (1987-1994), *Deep Space Nine* (1993-1999), *Voyager* (1995-2001) and *Enterprise* (2001-2005), and the feature films *The Motion Picture* (1979), *The Wrath of Khan* (1982), *The Search for Spook* (1984), *The Voyage Home* (1986), *The Final Frontier* (1989), *The Undiscovered Country* (1991), also *The Next Generation* films *Generations* (1994), *First Contact* (1996), *Insurrection* (1998) and *Nemesis* (2002).

Star Trek (now known as *Star Trek: The Original Series*) starred Montreal born William Shatner (Captain James T. Kirk), Leonard Nimoy (Mr. Spook) and DeForest Kelly ('Bones' McCoy).

William Shatner was born and raised in Montreal. He is most recognized for his starring role as Captain James T. Kirk on the science fiction series *Star Trek* (1966-1969) and for his portrayal of Sergeant Thomas Jefferson Hooker on the police drama series *T.J. Hooker* (1982-1986).

William Shatner also starred as government agent and master of disguise Jeff Cable in the ABC Television Network series *Barbary Coast* (1975-1976) co-starring Doug McClure. He was also the host of *Rescue 911* (1989-1996).

William Shatner directed episodes of *T.J. Hooker* as well as the motion picture *Star Trek: The Final Frontier*.

William Shatner has also written or co-written the following book series; *TekWar* series (9 books), *Star Trek* series (10 books), *War* series (2 books), *Quest for Tomorrow* series (5 books) and a series of non-fiction/autobiographies (7 books).

The science fiction *TekWar* book series were adapted to comic books, a video game and four made for television movies which would lead to the weekly television series *TekWar* (1994-1996) starring Greg Evigan and William Shatner, who also directed a few of the episodes. *TekWar* was filmed in Ontario and broadcast on the CTV Television Network.

In the ABC legal dramedies *The Practice* and *Boston Legal* (2004-2008), William Shatner portrayed attorney Denny Crane for which he won two Emmy Awards.

In 2000 William Shatner was inducted into Canada's Walk of Fame.

👆☺ April 17, 1969, Montreal Expos pitcher Bill Stoneman pitched a no hitter, beating the Philadelphia Phillies 7-0 at Connie Mach Stadium.

♦♠♥♣ I also enjoyed playing card games. *Go Fish, 52 Pickup, Solitaire* and *Rummy 500* were only a few of my favourites.

52 pick-up while not really a card game was played (as a practical joke) using a deck of 52 cards.

I would approach unsuspecting victims and asked if they wanted to play? If the 'victim' responded "Yes.", I would shuffle the deck of cards and then throw the deck high in the air, watch the cards splatter across the floor, and then tell the 'victim' to pick them up.

More often than not it would be me who would pick-up the deck of cards from the floor (because most people were not able appreciate a practical joke).

Author's Note:

Since my childhood years friends have asked me if I ever cheated while playing Solitaire. Of course I have! I play to win by any means necessary.

chapter two

Thrilled and excited, my older sister Ellen explains to my mother that she had caught a glimpse of John Lennon and Yoko Ono as they were leaving the Fairmont Queen Elizabeth Hotel on the final day of their much publicized 'Bed-In for Peace'.

In protest of the Vietnam War, John Lennon and his wife Yoko Ono (with her daughter Kyoko) staged two week long Bed-Ins for Peace, a week in Amsterdam and a week in Montreal.

Between May 26, 1969 to June 2, 1969, John Lennon and Yoko Ono granted interviews and conducted news conferences from their hotel bed for Peace. Their Peace Anthem 'Give Peace a Chance' (written by John Lennon) was recorded in room 1742, at the Queen Elizabeth Hotel.

My mother and sister both began reminiscing, when the Beatles (Paul McCartney, John Lennon, George Harrison and Ringo Starr) played two same day concerts (September 8th, 1964) at the Montreal Forum.

My mother purchased two tickets to the 4pm concert (the other concert was at 8:30pm). Both concerts were sold out. My bother George and I were babysat by my Auntie Carol.

My sister Ellen recalled that the music could hardly be heard because of the screaming fans. My mother explained that was what 'Beatlemania'. was all about, intense fan-frenzy.

Room 1742 at the Fairmont Queen Elizabeth Hotel is now known as the John Lennon and Yoko Ono Suite. The bedroom and living room of this Executive suite, is decorated with memorabilia of framed gold records, press clipping and photographs of John Lennon and Yoko Ono.

Also there's a collaborative work of Public Art on Mont Royal that reproduces 'Give Peace a Chance' in the 40 different languages spoken in Montreal.

Recollections, events, brief histories & trivia:

♪☺♫ The single 'Beautiful Second Hand Man' (1970) by popular Quebec singer Ginette Reno is receiving much airplay on both English and French radio stations.

Ginette Reno was born and raised in Montreal and has been a star in Quebec since the 1960's.

Ginette Reno released the hits 'Beautiful Second Hand Man' (1970), 'Des Croissants De Soleil' (1974). 'Un Peu Plus Haut Un Peu Plus Loin' (1975) The duet 'T'es Mon Amour, T'es Ma Maitresse' (1974) recorded with Jean-Pierre Ferland was played on both English and French radio stations.

Ginette Reno starred in the films *Léolo* (1992), *Mambo Italiano* (2000). Ginette Reno released the *Love Is All* (1998) album which contained the minor hit 'Hold On Heart'.

1982, Ginette Reno was made an Officer of the Order Of Canada and in 1999 was awarded the Governor General's Performing Arts Award.

In 2000 Ginette Reno was inducted into Canada's Walk of Fame.

🖊️😊🖌️ Attempting to copy or draw (not trace) the various characters from my Gold Key comic book collection.

I still have many of the drawings I drew as a child. I have often thought about compiling the drawings in a hard cover coffee table book and maybe title it, *Hommage to Gold Key*.

Maybe one day I'll do just that!

🎵🎶 The song 'You, Me and Mexico' (1970) by Toronto band Edward Bear is an international hit. Edward Bear would follow with the hits 'Masquerade' (1972), 'Last Song' (1972).

Singer and songwriter of Edward Bear, Larry Evoy would pursue a solo career and release the hit 'Here I Go Again' (1977).

👍😊 I would tune in every Saturday afternoon to watch CFCF 12's *Grand Prix Wrestling (1971-1975)*. Montreal radio and television personality Jack Curran was the ringside host.

Montreal has a long history and love for professional wrestling.

During the mid to late 1960's, wrestler Johnny Rougeau's *All-Star Wrestling* (French: *Les As De La Lutte*) was Quebec's main wrestling promotion, booking and selling out live events at both the Paul Sauvé Arena and the Montreal Forum.

Their wrestling show *Sur le Matelas* (English: *On The Mat*) aired weekly on CFTM Channel 10.

Popular wrestlers such as The Sheik, Gino Brito, Dino Bravo, Abdullah the Butcher, Jacques Rougeau Sr (Johnny Rougeau's brother), the Leduc brothers, (Joe and Paul) and cigar chomping wrestling manager Eddy 'the Brain' Creatchman worked for the *All-Star Wrestling* promotion. Eventually Jacques Rougeau's sons; Jacques Rougeau Jr. and Raymond Rougeau would join the promotion and become superstars.

During the early 1970's, wrestling brother's Paul 'the Butcher' Vachon and Maurice 'Mad Dog' Vachon, would create their own wrestling promotion *Grand Prix Wrestling* (French: *La Lutte Grande Prix*) and compete with its rival *All-Star Wrestling*, causing the first and only territorial war in the province. The popular Leduc brothers would leave *All-Star Wrestling* and join *Grand Prix Wrestling* for a more lucrative contract.

The 'Mormon Giant' Don Leo Johnathan joined *Grand Prix Wrestling* and slowing began a feud with a young 'Géant Jean Ferré' (Andre the Giant). Their feud would build for months until they finally met in an epic battle at a sold out Montreal Forum. A re-match of the 'Match of the Century' would soon follow, again to a sold out Montreal Forum.

High flying Édouard Carpentier's feuds with Walter 'Killer' Kowalski would be talked about for years to come.

*****

Unfortunately, in house bickering, wrestlers switching promotions, cash flow problems, controversy and scandals would take their toll on both wrestling promotions. By the end of 1975 both promotions had ceased operations.

Other wrestling promotions (*Celebrity Wrestling, Grand Circuit Wrestling*) tried to recreate the popularity of *All Star Wrestling* and *Grand Prix Wrestling* but to limited success.

Wrestler turned promoter Gino Brito's great and exciting *International Wrestling* would occupy the Montreal territory, selling out the Paul Sauvé Arena on a regular basis and also securing television deals in both official languages before losing key wrestlers to the *World Wrestling Federation* (aka World Wrestling Entertainment, WWE) in the mid nineteen eighties. The book *Mad Dogs, Midgets and Screw Jobs* written by Pat Laprade and Bertrand Hébert is a very insightful read about the history of wrestling in Montreal.

👍☺ November 1970, the Montreal Alouettes defeated the Calgary Stampeders 23-10 at Exhibition Stadium in Toronto to win their second Grey Cup.

👍☺ I enjoyed watching Graham Kerr in *The Galloping Gourmet*, a half-hour cooking show (1969-1971) taped in Ottawa and aired on the CBC.

Graham Kerr would open each show by leaping over a dining room chair, while holding a glass of wine in his hand.

The series would cease production in 1971 due to a near-fatal automobile accident involving Graham Kerr and his wife, Treena.

☺✍ It was while I was in the third grade, that I learned that I would need to wear prescription eye glasses.

The third grade teacher, Miss Douglas would seat her pupils (by family name) in alphabetical order. I found myself seated at the back of the classroom and not being able to see what the teacher had written on the blackboard.

I would make my way to the front of the classroom with pencil and notebook in hand to copy what was written, only to be told by my teacher to return to my seat.

Also in third grade, apparently because I was talking during class, I received the ruler from my teacher Miss Douglas. I was then sent down to the principal's office to explain my actions.

Back then, it was common practice for teachers to discipline their students by smacking both hands, palms open with a ruler and then being sent to the principal's office for more discipline i.e. the strap.

Standing at attention in front of the principal's office, his secretary (who had just notified him that I had been sent down by my teacher) would leave his office door ajar. I could see the principal removing his pants belt, folding the belt and then tapping it a few times in his hand. He would then open his office door, invite me in and close the door behind me.

The actual physical act or visual of being given the 'strap' was overshadowed by the sound of the belt smacking both my hands, palms open. 'Whack, whack, whack…Whack, whack!'

Miss Douglas would also throw chalk and/or the chalk brush at her pupils.

october crisis episode

I recall quite vividly, I must have been seven years old, it was mid-evening; my mother was wearing a housecoat standing in the doorway of the front balcony and looking towards the sky. I had gone towards her and asked what she was looking at.

I heard a loud sound, a motor? I also looked up to the sky and saw the sound I was hearing. It was an army helicopter flying overhead and the sound I heard was the helicopter propellers.

My mother responded that there was an army helicopter flying above and that I should return to my room. I asked her "Why?" She calmly told me to "Just do what you are told I'll be in soon to say goodnight." For a moment I felt there was more than just an army helicopter flying above. I did what I was told to do, I returned to my room.

It was only years later while I was attending junior high school, that the memory made sense to me. During a history class the teacher was discussing and trying to explain to his pupils the events of the October Crisis.

From 1963-1970 the Quebec Liberation Front (FLQ), engaged in terrorist acts and activities. Issuing declarations to overthrow the government of Quebec and calling for the independence of Quebec from Canada.

Numerous mailboxes were targeted and bombed. Other targets included recruitment offices, Montreal City Hall and the Montreal Stock Exchange.

1968, *'Trudeaumania'* was sweeping the nation. Pierre Elliot Trudeau's entry into the leadership race of the Liberal Party of Canada, garnered excitement among large fan bases who admired his socially liberal stances and were dazzled by his charm. His popularity was such that he would often be asked to sign autographs or be photographed.

Pierre Elliot Trudeau would go on to win the leadership of the Liberal Party of Canada and become the 15th Prime Minister of Canada.

October 1970, British Trade Commissioner James Cross is kidnaped. Quebec's Minister of Labour Pierre Laporte is also kidnapped and later executed. By request of the Canadian Government, military presence is sent to patrol the Montreal region.

When questioned by a CBC reporter, during an interview, on how far he was willing to go to stop the FLQ, Canadian Prime Minister Pierre Elliot Trudeau responded "Just watch me".

Former Quebec Cabinet Minister and founder of the Parti Québécois, René Lévesque strongly urges and advises both levels of government to negotiate with the FLQ.

Canadian Prime Minister Pierre Elliot Trudeau implements the War Measures Act, allowing wide-reaching powers to police, including the power to arrest and detain people without warrant.

December 1970, as a result of negotiations, British Trade Commissioner James Cross was freed by his captors who requested and received exile to Cuba.

There has since, been much debate and speculation as to whether then Canadian Prime Minister, Pierre Elliott Trudeau had gone too far, or had over reacted by sending the Canadian Army to patrol the streets of Montreal and in suspending the civil rights of Quebecers by implementing the War Measures Act.

Years later I questioned my mother about her thoughts and feelings concerning this dark period in Quebec history.

As a widowed mother of three children naturally she was confused and frightened. My mother responded quite frankly. "The FLQ were political terrorists, they made threats, bombed mail boxes and put the lives of citizens in jeopardy. The FLQ kidnaped James Cross; they not only kidnapped but later executed Pierre Laporte. No one individual was safe. Something had to be done and fast, to protect its citizens".

Episode Epilog:

When my mother heard on a CFCF 12 television newscast that the War Measure's Act had been implemented and the Canadian Army would be patrolling the streets of Montreal, (although she was still concerned and frightened) she felt a little more at ease and a little bit safer because of the actions taken by the Canadian Liberal Government and the army presence in the streets of Montreal.

chapter three

I have no recollections of my father Herbert because he had passed away when I was 18 months old. My father worked as a Taxicab driver and was a heavy drinker. I am told that he would drink from morning to night. He died from Cirrhosis of the liver. He was thirty-eight years old.

My older sister Ellen was spoiled and a goody two-shoes, always squealing on me and my brother George.

Recollections, events, brief histories & trivia:

👍😊 I remember anxiously waiting for the weekly *Fiesta Potato Chips* (French: Patate Fiesta) home delivery.

Fiesta Potato Chips would home deliver their products of assorted *Fiesta* brand flavoured soda pops and potato chips throughout the Province of Quebec.

Also, the *Fiesta Potato Chips* were packaged and concealed in a 1lb., 8 1/2" wide by 9 1/2" high circular tin can.

Fiesta Patato Chips were the freshest, crunchiest potato chip I have ever tasted.

👍😊 Snowball fights in the schoolyard.

🎵👍🎵 1971, the song 'Stay Awhile' by The Bells topped both the Canadian and American charts.

> The Bells were a Montreal band that enjoyed success with the hit records 'Moody Manitoba Morning' (1969 as The Five Bells), 'Fly Little White Dove Fly' (1970), 'Stay Awhile' (1970), 'For Better or Worse' (1971) and 'He Was Me He Was You' (1973).
>
> Some band members for The Bells included Cliff Edwards and his wife Ann Ralph (who had left the band to raise their family), Jackie Ralph, Doug Gravelle and Frank Mills.
>
> Cliff Edwards would leave the band to pursue a solo career in 1973, producing the hit single 'Carry On' credited to Cliff and Ann Edwards.
>
> Cliff Edwards would also star (with his wife Ann Edwards and brother Brian Edwards) in the half-hour, Montreal produced country-folk variety show, *The Cliff Edwards Show* (1974-1975) on CFCF Channel 12.
>
> Frank Mills was born in Montreal; (left The Bells in 1971) is a pianist and released the Canadian hits 'Love Me Love Me Love' (1971), 'Poor Little Fool' (1972), the instrumental 'Music Box Dancer' (1974) and the follow-up instrumental 'Peter Piper' (1979)

👍☺ 1971, watching a hockey game on television as Montreal Canadien's Captain Jean Beliveau scores three goals (hat-trick) including goal number 500 against Minnesota North Stars' rookie goaltender Gilles Gilbert.

I can still visualize the recently acquired (from the Detroit Red Wings) Frank Mahovlich skating up ice and passing the hockey puck to Phil Roberto who then passed the puck to Jean Beliveau.

During the 1970-1971 season, competing in the Stanley Cup Finals, the Montreal Canadiens (French: Les Canadiens de Montréal) would go on to defeat (in a best of seven series final 4-3) the Chicago Black Hawks and win their 17th Stanley Cup. Montreal Canadiens Captain Jean Beliveau would retire from hockey.

Due to friction between Montreal Canadiens head coach Al McNeil and some of the Montreal Canadiens players, winning the Stanley Cup would not be enough to save the coach's job.

Scotty Bowman would succeed Al McNeil as head coach of the Canadiens.

👆☺ Watching weekly on Saturday nights the music variety and video show *Like Young* hosted by Jim McKenna. *Like Young* was filmed in Montreal and produced at CFCF studios.

👆☺ We would also tune in each week to CFTM-Channel 10 (a French language television station) and watch popular Quebec host/ singer Pierre Lalonde on the French language music show *Jeunesse D'aujourd'hui.*

Jeunesse D'aujourd'hui (English: *Today's Youth*) (1962-1974) was a fun show to watch and a great showcase for French Quebec talent.

Although back then the recordings released were mostly French cover versions of the popular hits of the day, I remember such Quebec talent as Donald Lautrec singing the hit 'Eloise' (1969) Michelle Richard singing 'Les Boîtes À Gogo' (1966) Nicole Martin & Jimmy Bond 'On Est Fait Pour Vivre Ensemble' (1974) also Melody Stewart's 'La Vie Sans Toi' (1974) and 'Fio Mara Villa' (1974).

> The early seventies did produce a few artists who did write their own material such as singer/songwriter Marc Hamilton "Comme J'ai Toujours Envie D'aimer" (1970), Gilles Valiquette performing his classic Quebec hit songs 'Je Suis Cool' (1973) and 'La Vie En Rose' (1973).
>
> *****
>
> Host Pierre Lalonde would also release a series of hit records in both French; 'C'est le Temps des Vacances' (1963), 'Donne-moi ta Bouche' (1967), 'Louise' (1964), 'Quand Tu Viendras a Montréal' (1967)) and English; 'Louise' (1964), 'It's Gonna Be Cloudy' (1964) and 'We'll Have a Ball in Montreal' (1967).
>
> In later years Pierre Lalonde would host the game show *The Mad Dash* (1978-1985) and star in *The Pierre Lalonde Show*, a music variety show on CFCF Channel 12 and *Action Réaction* (1986-1991), a French language version of *Chain Reaction* on TQS.

👍😑 Participating in fistfights while playing street hockey with the neighbourhood kids.

👍😑 My sister Ellen began her first full-time job, working for an import/export company.

👍😑 Defending myself in the neighbourhood where I lived for being English speaking (although I was bilingual) in a predominantly French speaking district of the city.

👍😑 Watching the occasional episode of *The Pig and Whistle* (1967-1977) *The Pig and Whistle* was a weekly Canadian half-hour musical television series that was produced in Toronto by the CTV Television Network and aired on CFCF 12.

Set in a fictional British Pub and hosted by innkeeper John Hewer, *The Pig and Whistle* featured a mix of music, dance and comedy. The jovial Billy Meek was a regular on the show and the Canadian-Irish group, The Charlton Showband was the house band.

👍😊 Watching the CBC produced *The Irish Rovers Show* (1971-1975) on CBMT Channel 6 was a variety show of Irish folk songs and comedy.

The Irish Rovers were well known for their Canadian hit records 'The Unicorn' (1967), 'Wasn't That a Party' (1980) recorded as The Rovers and the Christmas recording of 'Grandma Got Run Over by a Reindeer' (1980).

👍😊 *The Ian Tyson Show* (1971-1975) was a half-hour country/folk music show, debuted as *Nashville North* (1970) in its first season, starred Canadian Ian Tyson, his then wife Sylvia and their band Great Speckled Bird.

Produced in Toronto by the CTV Television Network and aired on CFCF 12. Ian Tyson is best known for composing the song 'Four Strong Winds' and for his many duets recorded as Ian & Sylvia.

Ian Tyson released the romantic 'Springtime in Alberta' (1991).

In 1994, Ian Tyson became a Member of the Order of Canada and in 2003, received a Governor General's Award.

🎵👍🎵 The Five Man Electrical Band topped the Canadian charts with the songs 'Signs' (1971), and 'Absolutely Right' (1971).

Ottawa, Ontario band the Five Man Electrical Band would follow up their previous success with 'I'm a Stranger Here' (1972) and 'Werewolf' (1974).

Songwriter, singer and guitarist Les Emmerson would depart Five Man Electrical Band for a solo career and release the hit (while still a member of Five Man Electrical Band) 'Control of Me' (1972) and 'Cry Your Eyes Out' (1973).

🎵👍🎵 'Where Evil Grows' is a hit across Canada for the Poppy Family.

The Poppy Family were basically Terry Jacks, his then wife Susan Jacks and Craig McCaw; based in Vancouver, British Columbia the Poppy Family released the international hit 'Which Way You Going Billy?' (1969).

The Poppy Family disbanded in 1972 as the Jacks pursued solo careers and later divorced.

Susan Jacks was born in Saskatoon, Saskatchewan and released the solo hit 'You Don't Know What Love Is' (1973), 'I Thought Of You Again' (1973) 'I Want You To Love Me' (1974).

Singer/songwriter Terry Jacks was born in Winnipeg, Manitoba and released the solo hit 'Concrete Sea' (1972) 'Seasons In The Sun' (1974) 'If You Go Away' (1974) 'Rock and Roll (I Gave You The Best Years Of My Life)' (1975) 'Christina' (1975) 'Holly' (1975)

🎵👍🎵 Sunday afternoon's my mother would spend her day playing record albums and listening to Frank Sinatra, Dean Martin, Eddie Arnold and Tom Jones (she loved Tom Jones and was a member of his Fan Club).

My mother would be seated on the sofa next to the living room record player and sing along with the records.

🎵👍🎵 My sister Ellen would play the popular musical brands of the day; The British Invasion, Motown, Sonny and Cher and Gary Lewis & The Playboys.

*****

While my mother and sister Ellen enjoyed listening to various types of music; country, crooner, popular and Top 40, my brother George enjoyed listening to rock music and electric guitars.

George's favourite rock bands at that time were April Wine, Mahogany Rush, the Wackers and the Guess Who.

He used to drive my mother crazy playing the music a little louder than he should have.

April Wine was formed in Nova Scotia and relocated to Montreal in 1970. The band soon released their self-titled debut album on Aquarius Records (a record label founded in Montreal) and the single 'Fast Train' (1971) which received steady airplay on radio stations across Canada and in Montreal.

Despite numerous line-up changes over the years, songwriter, guitarist Myles Goodwyn would continue to front the rock band.

April Wine released many albums and bestselling singles including 'You Could Have Been a Lady' (1972), 'Lady Run, Lady Hide' (1972), 'Bad Side of the Moon' (1972), 'I Wouldn't Want to Lose Your Love' (1974), 'You Won't Dance with Me' (1977), 'Just Between You and Me' (1981), 'If You Believe in Me' (1993).

April Wine has always been one of Montreal's favourite rock bands.

****

The Wackers, an American band formed by Bob Segarini, and Randy Bishop (like April Wine) relocated to Montreal and released their second album *Hot Wacks* (1972) and a third album *Shredder* (1973) which included the hit single 'Day and Night' (1973). The band soon disbanded.

Randy Bishop released the single 'Don't You Worry' (1974) which received quite a bit of radio airplay throughout Canada, especially in Montreal.

*****

Mahogany Rush is a Montreal hard rock band, fronted by Jimi Hendrix inspired guitarist Frank Marino. Curiously, there has been a long standing myth that guitarist Frank Marino was visited by an apparition or the ghost of Jimi Hendrix, a myth that Frank Marino denies.

Mahogany Rush released their debut album *Maxoom* (1972) which contained the song 'Buddy'. The song 'Buddy' was a favourite of my brother George, he would play it constantly.

Montreal's rock radio station CHOM FM played the song 'Sister Change' (1979) from the album 'Tales of the Unexpected' (1979) regularly in its rotation. Frank Marino has also released a few solo albums.

*****

The Guess Who was a Canadian rock band from Winnipeg, Manitoba. Vocalist Burton Cummings and guitarist Randy Bachman were the group's primary songwriters, collaborating on the bands early hit records; 'These Eyes' (1968), 'Laughing' (1969) and 'Undun' (1969). The song 'American Woman' became an international hit (1970) and was followed by 'No Time' (1970) and 'No Sugar Tonight' (1970).

*****

Randy Bachman left the Guess Who in (1970) and formed the rock band Brave Belt which would eventually (with the addition of Winnipeg bassist/vocalist C.F. Turner) become Bachman-Turner Overdrive.

Bachman-Turner Overdrive would release many successful albums and numerous singles including the Canadian hits 'Let It Ride' (1974), 'You Ain't Seen Nothing Yet' (1974), 'Takin' Care of Business' (1974), 'Roll On Down The Highway' (1975) and 'Lookin' Out For #1' (1976).

*****

Burton Cummings continued to front the Guess Who through numerous personnel changes with continued success, scoring the hits 'Hand Me Down World' (1970), 'Share the Land' (1970), 'Clap for the Wolfman' (1974) (a tribute to legendary American disc jockey Wolfman Jack who lent his voice to the recording), 'Dancin' Fool' (1974) and 'Rosanne' (1975).

The Guess Who would soon disband (1975) when Burton Cummings decided to pursue a solo career.

In 2001 the Guess Who we're inducted to Canada's Walk of Fame.

In 1968, the Canadian Radio-television and Telecommunications Commission (CRTC) was created to enforce the Broadcast Act of Canada. Canadian content (CanCon) refers to the requirements that radio and television broadcasters must air a certain percentage of content partly written, produced, presented by persons from Canada.

The 'MAPL system' is the requirement used for music, In order to qualify as Canadian content a musical selection should fulfill at least two of the following conditions:

- M (the music is composed by a Canadian)
- A (the artist performing the music or the lyrics is Canadian)
- P (the performance is recorded or performed or broadcast live in Canada)
- L (the lyrics are written by a Canadian)

The 'MAPL' logo is a circle divided into four parts; one part for each of the 'MAPL' categories, and is easily recognized by Canadian radio stations as the logo appears on record album packaging and compact discs which increases the chance of the music receiving airplay in Canada.

The 'MAPL system' allowed the advancement and recognition of Canadian music talent. Talent we may have not known about if it were not for the Broadcast Act of Canada and the 'MAPL system'.

Canadian television programming has been difficult on the broadcasting industry. It is more economical for Canadian stations to purchase the Canadian broadcast rights to air an American series than it is to finance and produce a homemade production.

In English Canada, the public network CBC Television devotes the majority of its prime-time programming to Canadian content. While In Quebec, the French language networks (public and private) rely mostly on Canadian programming.

Much of the earlier Canadian programming was produced to fill or meet Canadian content requirements.

Canada is a diverse nation and an exciting country, the home grown talent is just as diverse and exciting.

chapter four

1972, my family experienced a big change to our lifestyle. We moved!

We left our downtown east end Cartier Street flat and moved a little bit north/east of the city to the Rosemount district. The change of scenery, (and the move) afforded my brother George and I to have our own bedrooms respectively.

For the first ten years of my life I shared a bedroom with George, (not that he was a terrible roommate) but it was nice to have my own space and privacy.

The move to Rosemount also allowed my mother to some much needed privacy.

The Cartier Street flat where we lived was basically three and a half rooms. One large room (where we were able to access the front balcony) was divided in two, by curtains hanging from the ceiling. The curtains were used as a divider or a wall.

My sister Ellen occupied one half of the room and my brother George and I occupied the other half. While my sister Ellen slept in a single bed, George and I shared a bunk bed. Nothing fancy just one bed frame atop of another bed frame.

My mother's sleeping quarters was the living room; she slept on a sofa bed. The third room was the kitchen and dining area and the half room was the bathroom. Well not really a bathroom, more like a toilet room. There was no bathtub or a shower, no wash basin either! We would wash ourselves in the kitchen area, at the kitchen sink.

So our move to the Rosemount district of Montreal was very welcome.

Recollections, events, brief histories & trivia:

👍☺ I was promoted to the fourth grade, and because my family moved to a different district, I was enrolled in another school. I was nervous my first day at the new school.

👍☺ Playing Dodge ball in the school yard during school recess

👍☺ Trading baseball and hockey cards with my new school friends.

👍☺ Because my family lived in close proximity to my new elementary school, I was happy to walk to and from school.

👍☺ Going to the neighbourhood *Depanneur Perrette* (a family run chain of corner convenience stores) for a refreshing bottle of *KIK Cola* (the champagne of colas), or an *Uptown* lemon soda, or even better a bottle of *Teem* lemon/lime soda.

👍☺ I watched a few televised games of the 1972 Summit Series, Canada-USSR.

Alan Eagleson, then National Hockey League Players Association executive director, negotiated an eight-game, best-of series tournament between the Soviet National Team and Canada's top professional players.

The first four games of the 1972 Summit Series were held in Canada and the remaining four games in Moscow. Both the CBC and CTV Television Networks shared broadcasting duties.

The '72 Summit Series was marred with controversy, bad penalty calls and questionable officiating.

During a two week hiatus between games four and five, Team Canada travelled to Sweden and played two exhibition games, winning the first game (4-1) and tying the second (4-4).

Entering into the eighth and final game of the tournament, with the series tied at three games and a tie, millions of Canadians tuned in to watch the historic deciding game.

At the start of the third period, with Team Canada down by two goals, Phil Esposito scored to bring Team Canada to within one goal.

Yvan Cournoyer would also score to even the game, or did he? The goal judge did not put the goal light on.

Alan Eagleson who was seated across the ice from the Team Canada bench, was furious and caused a ruckus in protest. While Alan Eagleson was being subdued or arrested by the Soviet police, Team Canada players and coaches rushed to his aid. Pete Mahovlich confronted the Soviet police with his hockey stick. Alan Eagleson was eventually freed and escorted to the Team Canada bench. Yvan Cournoyer's goal was allowed and the game was tied even at five.

With 34 seconds left to play in the third period, Paul Henderson recovered the rebound of a Phil Esposito shot on Soviet net minder Vladislav Tretiek.

With Vladislav Tretiek down on the ice, Paul Henderson scored the game winning goal.

Paul Henderson's 1972 Summit Series winning goal would become known as the Goal of the Century.

Summit Series '72 :

- September 02, 1972: **Soviet Union 7** – Canada 3
- September 04, 1972: **Canada 4** – Soviet Union 1
- September 06, 1972: **Canada 4** – Soviet Union 4
- September 08, 1972: **Soviet Union 5** – Canada 3
- September 22, 1972: **Soviet Union 5** – Canada 4
- September 24, 1972: **Canada 3** – Soviet Union 2
- September 26, 1972: **Canada 4** – Soviet Union 3
- September 28, 1972: **Canada 6** – Soviet Union 5

After defeating the Soviets, Team Canada played a final exhibition game in Czechoslovakia. The game would end in a 3-3 tie.

The book *Face-Off at the Summit* (1973) written by Team Canada goaltender Ken Dryden with Mark Mulvoy is an insightful, personal account of the 1972 Summit Series.

Another good read and personal account of the 1972 Summit Series is *Hockey Showdown* (1972) written by Team Canada's Head Coach Harry Sinden.

In 2012, Team Canada 1972 was inducted to Canada's Walk of Fame.

♪♫ Valdy is topping the Canadian music charts with the hit 'Rock & Roll Song' (1972).

Valdy was born in Ottawa, Ontario is a folk and country musician would also top the Canadian music charts with 'A Good Song' (1973), 'Yes I Can' (1976).

Valdy was appointed a member of the Order of Canada in 2011.

☹ 1972, the Montreal Expos traded Rusty Staub to the New York Mets.

I remember radio station CJAD's then morning man George Balcan announce that popular Montreal Expos right fielder Rusty Staub (also known as *'Le Grand Orange'*), was dealt to the New York Mets, in a shocking blockbuster trade for first baseman Mike Jorgensen, outfielder Ken Singleton and shortstop Tom Foli.

It was a sad day for Montreal and a sad day for Expos fans.

👍☺ Nancy Greene, a Canadian champion alpine skier appeared in *Mars Bar* commercials on television, proclaiming that "Mars bar makes a great break."

Nancy Greene was born in Ottawa (1943) and raised in British Columbia. As Canada's top skier through the 1960's, Nancy Greene won 17 Canadian Championship titles, and won silver and gold medals at the 1968 Grenoble Olympics.

Nancy Greene retired at the age of 24. Nancy Greene is married, and Mother to twin boys.

In 1999 Nancy Greene was named Canada's Athlete of the Century, and in 2009 took a seat as a Conservative member of the Senate of Canada.

👍☺ Rushing home during the school lunch hour, to watch two of my favourite cartoons *The Flintstones* and *Spider-Man* on CFCF Channel 12.

👍☺ October 2, 1972, Montreal Expo's starting pitcher Bill Stoneman pitches a second no-hit game beating the New York Mets 7-0 at Montreal's Jarry Park.

👍☺ Montreal Canadiens win their 18th Stanley Cup.

1972/73 season, The Montreal Canadiens beat the Chicago Black Hawks (in a best of seven series final 4-2) to win their 18th Stanley Cup.

This would be the first Stanley Cup win for Montreal Canadiens head coach Scotty Bowman.

🎵👍🎵 The cheerful 'Make My Life a Little Bit Brighter' (1973) by Canadian band Chester is a hit on Canadian radio stations.

🎵👍🎵 One of my all-time favourites, 'Pretty Lady' (1973) by Lighthouse is topping the charts.

Lighthouse is a Canadian band formed in Toronto, Ontario by vocalist/drummer Skip Prokop in 1968.

Lighthouse recorded the hit records '(Hat's Off) To The Stranger' (1971), 'One Fine Morning' (1971), 'Sunny Days' (1972), 'You Girl' (1973) and 'Pretty Lady' (1973).

👍☺ Secretariat won the 1973 Canadian International Stakes.

Secretariat, one of the greatest Thoroughbred racehorses of all time wins the 1973 Canadian International Stakes at Woodbine Racetrack in Toronto, Ontario.

The Canadian International Stakes would be the final race for Secretariat.

Secretariat (1970-1989) was trained by French Canadian Lucien Laurin (for the Meadow Farm Stable) and ridden mainly by Canadian jockey Ron Turcotte, although veteran jockey Eddie Maples rode Secretariat in its last race.

Ron Turcotte, was born (1941) in Grand Falls, New Brunswick and is a French Canadian thoroughbred race horse jockey.

Lucien Laurin (1912-2000) was born in Joliette, Quebec and began thoroughbred horse racing as a jockey at Blue Bonnets Raceway in Montreal, Quebec.

*****

Blue Bonnets opened in 1907 on Decarie Boulevard in Montreal and featured thoroughbred horse racing until 1954 (which later resumed in 1961and again ended in 1975). In 1943 harness racing was introduced to Blue Bonnets.

From 1961 to 1975 Blue Bonnets was home to the Quebec Derby, an annual Canadian thoroughbred horse race.

In 1995, Blue Bonnets was renamed Hippodrome de Montreal and featured harness racing, off-track betting, video lottery terminals and slot machines. In 2009 the race track was permanently closed.

*****

In 1971, Lucien Laurin began working for the Meadow Farm Stable where he trained their colt Riva Ridge (1969-1985), winning the Kentucky Derby and Belmont Stakes (with jockey Ron Turcotte) in 1972.

Despite their success with Riva Ridge, Lucien Laurin is better known as the trainer and Ron Turcotte as the jockey for Secretariat who in 1973 would become the first Triple Crown (in the U.S. the three races that make up the Triple Crown are the Kentucky Derby, Preakness Stakes and the Belmont Stakes) winner in twenty-five years.

****

The 1973 Canadian International Stakes at Woodbine Race Tracks in Toronto, Ontario, was the final race that Secretariat would compete in and win.

Ron Turcotte's career ended in 1978 when at the start of a race he took a tumble from his horse that left him a paraplegic.

Lucien Laurin and Ron Turcotte are both inducted into the National Museum of Racing and Hall of Fame.

Lucien Laurin passed away in 2000.

Walt Disney Films released the film Secretariat (2010) starring Diane Lane and John Malkovich.

👍😊 Watching *The Starlost* (1973-1974)

The Starlost starred Kier Dullea, Gay Rowan and Robin Ward.

The Starlost was a low budget hour long science fiction series that was produced in Toronto by the CTV Television Network and aired on CFCF Channel 12.

🎵🎶 The perfect 'A Touch of Magic' (1973) by James Leroy and Denim was a huge hit across Canada.

Ontario band James Leroy and Denim would also release the Canadian hit 'Make it all Worthwhile' (1973).

James Leroy committed suicide in 1979.

👍☺ I watched a few televised games of the 1974 Summit Series, Canada-USSR.

> The CBC and CTV Television Networks televised a second Summit Series. The 1974 Summit Series featured a Canadian team represented by the World Hockey Association competing against the Soviet Team.
>
> The first four games of the 1974 Summit Series were held in Canada and the remaining four games in Moscow.
>
> Resembling the 1972 NHL Summit Series, the 1974 WHA Summit Series would also be marred with controversy, bad penalty calls and questionable officiating.
>
> The WHA Canadian team would lose the eight game series with 1 win, 4 losses and 3 ties.
>
> ## Summit Series '74:
>
> - September 17, 1974: Canada 3 – USSR 3
> - September 19, 1974: **Canada 4** – USSR 1
> - September 21, 1974: **USSR 8** – Canada 5
> - September 23, 1974: Canada 5 – USSR 5
> - October 01, 1974: **USSR 3** – Canada 2
> - October 03, 1974: **USSR 5** – Canada 2
> - October 05, 1974: USSR 4 – Canada 4
> - October 06, 1974: **USSR 3** – Canada 2

****

The World Hockey Association (French: Association Mondiale de Hockey) (1972-1979) tried to capitalize on a lack of Canadian and American professional hockey teams by expanding and offering hockey franchises in key cities, and also to attract players as an alternative to the National Hockey League by paying the players more than the National Hockey League owners would.

The World Hockey Association also signed European players to play in their hockey league.

Led by Chicago Black Hawks star forward Bobby Hull, (who had signed a $2.75 million, ten year contract with the WHA's Winnipeg Jets) more than sixty players jumped from the NHL to the WHA.

A retired 'Mr. Hockey' Gordie Howe would sign with the WHA's Houston Aeros, allowing him the opportunity to play hockey with his two sons Mark and Marty.

*****

Unfortunately the World Hockey Association would be plagued with problems. Many teams experienced financial difficulties, folding or moving from one city to another (sometimes in mid-season). Low attendance and player salaries also attributed to the leagues financial difficulties.

During its final season, unable to meet payrolls and other financial difficulties the WHA merged with the NHL in 1979.

Four of the six remaining WHA teams, the Winnipeg Jets, Quebec Nordiques, Edmonton Oilers and the New England Whalers (renamed the Hartford Whalers) joined the NHL.

The National Hockey League would treat the merger as an expansion and refused to recognize any WHA hockey league records or statistics.

*****

Montreal Canadiens great Maurice Richard briefly coached the WHA Quebec Nordiques (two games; a loss and a win before realizing he did not have the temperament to be a full time coach) during their first season (1972-1973).

Another Montreal Canadiens great, goaltender Jacques Plante also coached the WHA Quebec Nordiques (1973-1974).

During the 1976-1977 seasons the WHA Quebec Nordiques would defeat the Winnipeg Jets in a best of seven game series (4-3) and win the WHA Avco World Trophy or Avco Cup.

Future Montreal Canadiens Stanley Cup winning coach, Jacques Demers (1992-1996) coached the WHA Quebec Nordiques during their final season (1978-1979) in the World Hockey Association and also during their first season (1979-1980) in the National Hockey League.

In 2009, Jacques Demers took a seat as a Conservative member of the Senate of Canada.

The Quebec Nordiques would become provincial rivals to the Montreal Canadiens.

A seventeen year old Wayne Gretzky would appear in eight games for the WHA Indianapolis Racers before being traded to the WHA Edmonton Oilers.

Wayne Gretzky would become one of the greatest hockey players of all-time.

Ed Willes wrote the informative book *The Rebel League: The Short and Unruly Life of the World Hockey Association* (2005).

👆☺ *The Amazing World of Kreskin* (1970-1975) produced in Ottawa by CTV and aired on CFCF 12 was a half hour show that showcased Kreskin's mental and intuitive abilities.

I had seen a few episodes and was quite impressed with Kreskin's "predictions".

👆☺ November 1974, The Montreal Alouettes beat the Edmonton Eskimos 20-7 at Empire Stadium in Vancouver to win their third Grey Cup.

🎵👆🎵 The song '(You're) Having My Baby' (1974) a duet by Canadian singer/songwriter Paul Anka with Odia Coates is an international hit.

> Canadian singer/songwriter Paul Anka was born in Ottawa, Ontario and gained fame during the late 1950's when (while still a teen-ager) he wrote and recorded the timeless classics, 'Diana' (1956), 'You Are My Destiny' (1957), 'Lonely Boy' (1958) 'Put Your Head On My Shoulder' (1959), 'Time To Cry' (1959) and 'Puppy Love' (1959).
>
> Paul Anka wrote 'It Doesn't Matter Anymore' (1958), for Buddy Holly who recorded the song before his tragic death in a plane crash (February 1959).
>
> 'Tutti's Trumpets' recorded the pop instrumental 'Toot Suite (It's Only Love)' (1959) composed by Paul Anka who added lyrics to the song for Annette Funicello version, 'Its Really Love' (1959).
>
> In 1962, 'Toot Suite (It's Only Love)' was given a new arrangement and would become the theme music (Johnny's Theme) for *The Tonight Show* starring Johnny Carson.

During the 1960's Paul Anka continued to write and record. Paul Anka wrote the English lyrics to 'My Way' (1967) recorded by Frank Sinatra. He also wrote 'She's a Lady' (1971) for Tom Jones and co-wrote with Michael Jackson the song 'This Is It' (2009).

1974, Paul Anka guest starred as an informant who uses a detective to further his criminal career on the CBS police drama series *Kojak* starring Telly Savalas.

During the mid-1970's, Paul Anka wrote and produced the Don Goodwin singles 'This Is Your Song' (1973) and the remake hit 'Time To Cry' (1974).

Also during the seventies Paul Anka had a string of hit records including '(Your) Having My Baby' (1974), 'I Don't Like to Sleep Alone' (1974), 'One Man Woman' (1974), '(I Believe) There's Nothing Stronger Than Our Love' (1975) all were recorded with Odia Coates.

*****

Odia Coates was an American singer who is best remembered for her duets recorded with Paul Anka. Her fantastic self-titled debut album was produced by Paul Anka and featured the hit singles 'You Come And You Go' (1975) and 'Don't Leave Me In The Morning' (1975).

Odia Coates passed away in 1991.

*****

Paul Anka recorded the fantastic *Walk A Fine Line* (1983) album and released the huge hit 'Hold Me 'Til The Morning Comes' (1983).

Paul Anka has successfully continued to tour and record.

****

There is a street in the city of Ottawa named Paul Anka Drive. In 2005, Paul Anka was inducted into Canada's Walk of Fame. In 2013, the book *My Way* an autobiography written by Paul Anka with David Dalton was released.

Author's Note:

Paul Anka is the perfect performer in a class all his own. I went to a Paul Anka show/concert at Place des Arts (a major performing arts centre in Montreal) during the 1980's To this day the Paul Anka concert I attended is fondly remembered and considered to be one of my all-time favourite shows.

👍😊 *Mr. Chips* (1973-1979 was a weekly, half-hour home improvement and carpentry show filmed at CFCF Studio in Montreal.

I enjoyed watching Bill Brown (aka *Mr. Chips*) with his assistant Don McGowan; demonstrate to viewers how to do home repairs and basic carpentry.

Mr. Chips also aired on the CBC Television Network.

🎶👍🎵 Winnipeg, Manitoba band Bachman–Turner Overdrive is rocking the radio airwaves with the hits 'Let It Ride' (1974), 'You Ain't Seen Nothing Yet' (1974) and 'Takin' Care of Business' (1974).

👍😊 *The Ronnie Prophet Show* (1974) was a CBC television music variety show that was broadcast on CBMT Channel 6.

The Ronnie Prohet Show was an eleven week summer replacement for CBC's long running *The Tommy Hunter Show (1965-1992)*.

Ronnie Prophet previously hosted the CBC country music television series *Country Roads* (1973).

A talented musician and singer, Ronnie Prophet's 'Harold the Horny Toad' routine is hilarious.

👍☹ I brought my mother to a Saturday matinee viewing of *Why Rock The Boat?* starring Stuart Gillard as a cub reporter at the *Atwater Theatre* in the Alexis Nihon Plaza.

Set in 1940's Montreal *Why Rock the Boat?,* is a romantic comedy about the misadventures of cub reporter Harry Barnes who lands his first job and falls in love with a female reporter from a rival newspaper.

Why Rock The Boat? is based on the best-selling book of the same name written by Montreal author William Weintraub.

A Canadian journalist, author and filmmaker for Canada's National Film Board, William Weintraub was born, raised and educated in Montreal.

His experience as a journalist would provide the basis for his novel *Why Rock the Boat?* (1961)

Other books written by William Weintraub include *The Underdogs* (1979), *City Unique* (1996) and *Crazy About Lili* (2005).

Crazy About Lili is a coming of age story. Richard Lippman is attending his first year of university, when his uncle introduces Richard to Lili L'Amour, the striptease queen.

William Weintraub was made an Officer of the Order of Canada in 2003.

👍☺ A Canadian version to the highly successful American country television variety show *Hee-Haw* (1969-1997) was CTV's weekly half hour *Funny Farm* (1974-1975).

Blake Emmons was the host and actress Jayne Eastwood from Toronto, Ontario was a series regular.

👍☺ My mother and I would tune in weekly to watch the locally produced television sitcom *Excuse My French* (1974-1976) on CFCF 12.

Stuart Gillard and Lisa Charbonneau starred for two seasons as a mixed, Quebec Anglophone and Quebec Francophone, couple living in Montreal.

The comedy series dealt with the couple's daily struggles and the language issue in Quebec, (two points of view, the Anglophone and Francophone), and the friction within their extended families.

Author's Note:

Born and raised in Montreal and although I am bilingual, I would also have to deal with and come to terms with, and eventually arrive to the conclusion that for better or worse there will always be (regardless of what political party may be governing Quebec) a language issue in the Province of Quebec.

*****

👍☺ I enjoyed watching the beautiful Diane Severson bump, elbow, hit and knock down her opponents on the weekly televised *Roller Derby* (1974).

I enjoyed watching *Roller Derby* (1974) a weekly Roller Game was presented, featuring different Roller Derby Teams in competition.

Although I did not understand the rules of the sport, it was fun to watch the two opposing team's race around a track, bumping, crashing and fighting, all the while trying to hinder the opposing team's 'jammer', while helping their team's 'jammer'. 'A 'jammer' is a designated scoring player.

The Canadian All Stars (also known as the Canadian Braves) Women's Team were my favourite to watch. Roller Derby stars Gwen 'Skinny Minnie' Miller and Diane Severson were always the crowd favourites.

The Roller Derby, Roller Game of the week was televised on CFCF 12, hosted by Barry Dale and Aaron Rand who also provided the 'play by play'.

Aaron Rand is a Montreal institution, a legend (afternoon drive at CFCF 600) an icon (morning man at CFQR 92.5 FM, Q92) and CJAD 800 in English radio.

Montreal has had some great and legendary radio announcers and disk jockeys. The talent that has graced Montreal airwaves is simply incredible.

A few voices and a few names that I had the pleasure of listening to come to mind;

- Dave Boxer - CJFM (FM 96)
- Jack Finnigan - 98 CKGM, CJAD 800 Trivia Show
- Dave Fisher - CJAD 800 Trivia Show
- Dean Hagopian - CJFM (FM 96) Morning Show
- George Balcan - CFCF 600, CJAD 800 Morning Show

- Mark Burns - 98 CKGM News, CJFM (FM 96) Morning Show
- Ralph Lockwood - 98 CKGM Morning Show
- Aaron Rand & Tasso Patsikakis (aka. Paul Zakaib) - CFCF 600 Afternoon Drive, CFQR 92.5 FM Morning Show, Q92 Morning Show
- Jim Bay - 98 CKGM Morning Sports
- Dan Wilmont - 98 CKGM Evenings
- Andrew Carter - CHOM 97.7 FM Morning Show, CJAD 800 Morning Show
- Terry Dimonte & Ted Bird - CHOM 97.7 FM Morning Show, Mix 96 Morning Show, CJAD 800 Morning Show
- Marc Denis - 98 CKGM, Le <u>Décompte</u> CKOI FM, Q92 Saturday Night Oldies, AM 940 Morning Show
- Bill Roberts - 98 CKGM Morning News
- Robert G. Hall - 98 CKGM Mid-Morning
- Tommy Schnurmacher - CHOM 97.7 FM Entertainment, CJAD 800 Mid-Morning
- Daniel Feist - CJFM (FM 96) Rhythms International, Mix 96 Rhythms International
- Ted Tevan - CFCF 600 Sports Rap
- Alain Montpetit - 98 CKGM News, CKLM FM Evenings, CKMF FM Morning Show, CFQR 92.5 FM Morning Show

*****

Alain Montpetit was born and raised in Westmount, (an on-island suburb of Montreal) Quebec. Alain Montpetiti has worked in both English and French radio and television.

During the 1970's he worked at Montreal am radio station 98 CKGM as an air staffer/reporter and as the morning man at French radio station CKLM.

It was while working at French radio station CKMF FM 94.3 where he hosted the successful 'Le 5 à 8' show, a disco music radio show (the disco era was at its most popular) and also while hosting the very popular disco dance show *Et Ça Tourne*, on the French TVA Television Network, that he would become one of the biggest radio announcers and television personalities in Quebec.

Alain Montpetit would also become known as the 'King of Disco' (and as a 'jet-setter', moving between Montreal's and New York's social scenes) receiving and accepting (according to news reports) payment (in cash or drugs) from various nightclub owners for appearances he would make at their establishments.

Alain Montpetit co-hosted the French afternoon talk show *Midi-Soleil* (1985) with Louis-Josée Mondoux and was the host of the French game show *Odyssée* (1984-1985).

Alain Montpetit also continued to work in radio becoming morning man at English radio station CFQR FM 92.5 and French radio's CKMF FM 94.3, where he was fired (June 1987) and physically removed from the station for being under the influence as he had been on previous occasions.

In July 1987 Alain Montpetit was found dead of an apparent drug overdose in a Washington hotel room.

****

In 2002, New York City police reinvestigated the brutal 1982 murder of a rising French-Canadian (Montreal born) fashion model. The model, was active in the New York and Montreal nightlife, had been stabbed repeatedly in her New York City apartment.

A neighbour who saw the model walking with a man hours before the murder, helped a police sketch artist produce a drawing that resembled Alain Montpetit.

Cold case detectives also revealed that two women, told investigators that Alain Montpetit had confessed his guilt to them. Also a former girlfriend of Alain Montpetit recanted previous statements that he had been with her at the time of the murder.

Investigators believed that following a party at the Xenon, (a trendy discotheque) Alain Montpetit became enraged when the Montreal model rejected his request to help him renew a relationship with a friend of hers.

*****

The bilingual Quebec film *Funkytown* (2011) written by Steve Galluccio and directed by Daniel Roby was filmed and set in Montreal during the height of the disco era (1976-1980).

Montreal actor and comedian Patrick Huard portrays a fictionalised version of Alain Montpetit.

chapter five

I graduated from elementary school and began attending Junior High School or Secondary School (French: école secondaire). I was also growing (both physically and mentally) as a human being, becoming more mature and independent.

My teen-age years would define the man that I would become, mentally, socially, economically and politically. Although I shared in many friendships, I was basically (and still am) a loner.

My mother budgeted as best as she could on a fixed (widow's pension) monthly income. She would give both my brother George and I, (my sister Ellen was gainfully employed and contributing monetarily to the household) an allowance of two dollars a week for chores we would do.

During the cold winter months we would shovel snow off of the front and back balconies or sweep the entrance of the flat (duplex) where we lived. We would clean the dishes after every meal, and put out the garbage for collection.

It was during this time (1975) that Joe a school friend asked if I would be interested in working a part-time job as a busboy/dishwasher. Joe explained that his older brother was working the part-time job but was leaving for another job. I asked Joe why he didn't want the job and he simply responded that he didn't want to work.

The employment would be one day a week, on weekends, five hours, working at a restaurant, near the Montreal Forum, downtown. I would be paid for the hours I worked. I was so excited!

Although my mother was apprehensive and concerned with my grades at school, I tried my best to convince her to let me work that one day, part-time. I explained that working on a part-time basis would not affect my grades and that I could use the salary (I would earn) to buy for myself what she could not.

I continued to press and plead with her until she finally agreed. My mother even wrote a permission to work letter for my first and new employer.

The *Texan Restaurant* was situated on the corner of Ste. Catherine and Closse Street, a block away from the Montreal Forum, had been a Montreal fixture for many years. Famous for being a family style restaurant, its Southern style chicken and hamburgers in the basket were Montreal favourites.

The owner Mister George was a kind and generous man, the service personnel, prompt and courteous and the kitchen staff friendly and professional. The menu was great, the food served was incredible and the atmosphere boisterous, especially on game nights.

Hockey nights at the Montreal Forum meant very busy evenings to the *Texan Restaurant*.

Before and after hockey games, the *Texan Restaurant* would be full to capacity with dining customers. Outside, line ups of people would be waiting to be welcomed and served.

A who's who of Montreal sport and television personalities would frequent the *Texan Restaurant*. Sport columnist Red Fisher would be seen sharing a table with CFCF 12 sportscaster Dick Irvin.

Many of the Montreal Canadian's Hockey players would also drop in for a quick bite before or after games.

I was originally scheduled to work on Sunday's, the 8am-4pm shift. Eventually I would work twenty-five hours a week (during a school week) and forty hours during the summer break from school.

Although at first I was nervous and lacking a little in self-confidence, I was a quick learner.

I soon realized and understood the benefits and importance of this employment. I was now able to afford myself what my two dollar a week allowance couldn't.

Because my mother was on a fixed monthly income (a widow's pension), it was sometimes difficult for her to afford her children the necessities that she would have liked to provide. Often I was given my older brother's (hand-me-down) clothes to wear, simply because my mother was unable to purchase two new items of clothing.

On many occasions I asked my mother to loan me an advance on my allowance (most often she was unable to) so that I would be able to go to the movie theater with my friends.

Working part-time at the *Texan Restaurant* allowed and enabled me to purchase what my mother was not able to afford.

Recollections, events, brief histories & trivia:

$©$ Accompanied by my mother, I opened a savings account at my local banking institution *The Montreal City and District Savings Bank*.

☝☺ Shopping at the local *Woolworth* (a chain of general merchandise stores) and *Rossy* (a chain of variety stores).

$©$ I bought myself a General Electric brand, am/fm Alarm Clock Radio.

I use to listen to AM radio station 98 CKGM. Morning man, Ralph 'Birdman' Lockwood was extremely funny, full of energy and bad jokes. I enjoyed him so much. "How's your oiseau?" he would ask his listeners.

I still remember his television commercials for *Dorion Suits* (French: *Aux Habits Dorion*) and of course who could forget the *Bar B- Barn* chicken and ribs commercials?

98 CKGM's Top 40 music format was complimented by its on-air radio announcers.

My favourite 98 CKGM radio announcers included, Robert G. Hall, Marc 'Mais Oui' Denis, 'Big' Dan Willmott and morning news anchor Bill Roberts. 98 CKGM and its radio announcers were always there to keep me company.

98 CKGM is a part of Montreal radio history that I miss to this day.

👍🙂 I was able to treat myself to some entertainment by going to the various movie theatres in Montreal, such as the *Palace Theatre* on St. Catherine, the *Atwater Theatre* in the Alexis Nihon Plaza.

👍🙂 I also attended the final showing of the Steven Spielberg Motion Picture *Jaws* (1975) starring Roy Scheider, Richard Dreyfuss and Robert Shaw at the *Lowe's Theatre* on St. Catherine Street.

🏈☹🏈 November 23, 1975, the Edmonton Eskimos beat the Montreal Alouettes 9-8 to win the Grey Cup at McMahon Stadium in Calgary.

chapter six

Wednesday December 31, 1975, New Year's Eve I was working
at the *Texan Restaurant*. I normally worked on Sunday but that
evening was an exception as The Montreal Canadiens were to face
off against the Central Red Army at the Montreal Forum.

Super Series '76 was a series of eight exhibitions games,
the National Hockey League would play against two touring
teams, Central Red Army and Soviet Wings, from the Soviet
Championship League.

Eight National Hockey League teams would compete against
the two Soviet teams. The Central Red Army would face off
against four NHL teams as would the Soviet Wings.

With two games already played (Central Red Army beat the
New York Rangers and the Soviet Wings beat the Pittsburgh
Penguins) the Central Red Army were to meet the Montreal
Canadians for game three of the eight game series.

The *Texan Restaurant* was busy the whole evening, with a line-up
of people waiting patiently outside for their turn to enter the
restaurant. I had worked during hockey nights and a few concert
nights at the Forum but that night was exceptionally busy.

The kitchen and service staff did their best to serve and 'put out' the food orders as fast as possible, as many customers were to attend the hockey game.

In the kitchen was a transistor radio broadcasting the hockey game. Although we were extremely busy we were able to hear bits and pieces of the broadcast, exchanging among ourselves what we had heard. The hockey game would end in a 3-3 tie.

We did not know it at the time but the hockey match-up between the Montreal Canadiens and the Central Red Army, would be discussed and written about for years to come as the greatest hockey game ever played.

Super Series '75-'76:

- December 28, 1975: **Red Army 7** - New York Rangers 3
- December 29, 1975: **Soviet Wings 7** - Pittsburgh Penguins 4
- December 31, 1975: Red Army 3 - Montreal Canadiens 3
- January 4, 1976: **Buffalo Sabres 12** - Soviet Wings **6**
- January 7, 1976: **Soviet Wings 4** - Chicago Black Hawks 2
- January 8, 1976: **Red Army 5** - Boston Bruins 2
- January 10, 1976: **Soviet Wings 2** - New York Islanders 1
- January 11, 1976: **Philadelphia Flyers 4** - Red Army 1

Recollections, events, brief histories & trivia:

$☺$ I was able to buy myself an audio cassette tape recorder and a Realistic brand Record Player, both from *Radio Shack*, presently known as *The Source/La Source*.

I remember the first time I went record shopping with my brother George. One Saturday morning we woke early and made our way to downtown rue St. Catherine.

Our first stop was *A&A Records* and then a little later to *Sam the Record Man*. We browsed the wall to wall record albums practically the whole day.

A&A Records was a Canadian record store chain and at one time was the dominant record store chain with stores throughout Canada. *A&A Records* declared bankruptcy in 1991.

Sam the Record Man was also a Canadian record store chain. *Sam the Record Man* would have fantastic blowout sales on Boxing Day. In 2001, due to tough competition, narrow profit margins and the availability of free music downloads from the Internet, *Sam the Record Man* declared bankruptcy.

I recall many a Boxing Day freezing with my brother George in a long line-up waiting for Sam the Record Man to open for business so we could purchase record albums.

Another record store we frequented often was the very relaxed and laid back *Phantasmagoria* on Park Avenue.

*****

$☺$ One of the first albums I purchased was the *K-tel International* 'themed' *Canadian Mint*, featuring popular Canadian

61

music artists of the day. I also purchased the K-tel International *'Record Selector'* to store my albums.

K-tel International was hugely successful during the 1970's, for its variously 'themed' music compilation record albums, its advertising campaigns 'As Seen On TV' and other non-music related ventures such as the *'Record Selector'* (to store and easily view Vinyl record albums) and the *'Dial-o-matic'*, a food slicer.

👍☺ Listening to Montreal Expos baseball on CFCF 600.

Working full-time at the *Texan Restaurant* during the summer months, my co-workers in the kitchen would always turn on the transistor radio and listen to Montreal Expo's Baseball on CFCF 600.

Dave Van Horne called the play by play while Duke Snider was the radio analyst. Dave Van Horne and Duke Snider were the greatest baseball announcers, and so much fun to listen to.

In my mind I can still hear the voice of Dave Van Horne calling a home run with his signature *"up, up and away"*.

👍☺ On more than one occasion I witnessed The Great Antonio tie a chain to a Montreal city bus and pull the bus loaded with passengers along St. Catherine Street.

Arriving in Canada in 1945, Antonio Barichievich was born October 10, 1925 in Croatia. Weighing over 400 pounds and standing 6 foot 4 inches tall.

The Great Antonio traveled and toured the world displaying, his feats of strength and is recorded in the Guinness Book of World Records.

In later years I would see the Great Antonio, at the Berri-UQAM metro station selling pictures of himself and brochures of his life story.

Sadly in 2003 Antonio Barichievich died of a heart attack.

chapter seven

My brother George graduated high school and began working full-time on the assembly line in a manufacturing. After a three month probation period he would become part of a labor union.

My sister Ellen, had begun dating and was rarely home

Mornings my mother would look forward to the Monday to Saturday home delivery of the English-language *Montreal Star* newspaper.

She would read the broadsheet size newspaper from front to back. The *Montreal Star* did not publish a Sunday newspaper. The weekly tabloid size *Sunday Express,* was home delivered.

Due to an eight month pressmen strike in 1978, (the French language tabloid *Montréal-Matin*, folded in1978) which resulted in a loss in advertising and readership to its rival English-language newspaper the *Montreal Gazette*, the *Montreal Star* ceased operations in September 1979.

The *Sunday Express* would cease operations in 1985.

The short-lived tabloid size *Montreal Daily News* was launched in 1988 and folded in 1989.

The *Montreal Gazette* remains the sole English-language newspaper published in Montreal.

My mother would spend the remainder of her mornings doing laundry, dusting, cleaning, and straitening up the flat.

She also used to go out every day, maybe for groceries or just window shopping. During the summer months my mother would sit in a chair on the front balcony, reading or just watching people walk by.

Early afternoons to mid-afternoons she would watch daytime programming including various game and talk shows.

👆😐 *It's Your Move* (1975-1979).

One of my mother's favourite game shows was then CFCF 600 radio morning man George Balcan hosting the daytime charades themed *It's Your Move* (1974-1975).

It's Your Move was filmed at the studios of CFCF 12 in Montreal.

Paul Hanover would continue to hosting *It's Your Move* (1975-1979) for the remainder of the show's run on CFCF 12.

George Balcan (1932-2004) was raised in Dauphin, Manitoba where he started his broadcasting career. George Balcan moved to Montreal in 1963, and began working as afternoon host on CJAD before becoming the station's morning man in 1967.

He would briefly work as morning man at cross-town competitor CFCF (1973-1975) and also hosted CFCF 12's afternoon movie show *Matinee* and the game show *It's Your Move* (1974-1975) before returning to CJAD in 1975 where he remained until his retirement in 1998.

George Balcan was also an accomplished pastel artist and was appointed a Member of the Order of Canada in 1996.

George Balcan passed away from cancer in 2004.

👍😊 *First Impressions* (1976-1977).

A panel of three couples, who were introduced prior to show time answered questions, based solely on their first impressions of their designated partners.

First Impressions was a half-hour daytime game show filmed at CFCF 12 in Montreal and was hosted by Alan Thicke.

👍😊 *The Mad Dash* (1978-1985).

The Mad Dash was hosted by the popular Pierre Lalonde and filmed at CFCF 12 in Montreal.

Two pairs of contestants compete in a life sized board game.

👍😊 *Super Pay Cards* (1981-1982).

Hosted by Art James with co-host Mary Lou Basaraba, *Super Pay Cards* was a poker themed game show where contestants played against each other to build poker hands from a board of 20 hidden cards.

Super Pay Cards was filmed in Montreal at CFCF 12.

👍😊 *Celebrity Cooks* (1975-1979).

Taped in Vancouver, the relaxed and fun to watch *Celebrity Cooks* was hosted by Bruno Gerussi and aired daily on the CBC Television Network.

Celebrity Cooks was a cooking/talk show in which host Bruno Gerussi would interview and chat with various celebrity guests while preparing food.

Bruno Gerussi was also the star of the long running CBC comedy/drama *The Beachcombers* (1972-1990).

Bruno Gerussi passed away from a heart attack in 1995.

👆☺ *The Alan Hamel Show* (1976-1980).

The Alan Hamel Show was a daily one hour afternoon talk show produced in Vancouver by the CTV Television Network and aired on CFCF 12.

My mother enjoyed the interviews and the friendly banter between Alan Hamel and his guests.

> Canadian Alan Hamel was born in Toronto, Ontario and hosted the half-hour, CBC children's show *Razzle Dazzle* (1962-1964).
>
> Alan hosted the *Anniversary Game* (1969-1970), a daily American syndicated game show. Aspiring actress Suzanne Somers was one of the prize models during the show's run.
>
> Alan Hamel was host of his popular afternoon daily talk show *The Alan Hamel Show*. Alan Hamel married *Three's Company* actress Suzanne Somers in 1977 and became her manager.

👆☺ *Mantrap* (1971-1972) was a daily half-hour panel show hosted by Alan Hamel and produced in Vancouver by the CTV Television Network. Suzanne Somers was a frequent guest panellist.

👆☺ *Alan Hamel's Comedy Bag* (1972-1973) was a variety comedy series filmed in Montreal, produced by the CBC and aired on CBMT Channel 6.

👆☺ *The Alan Thicke Show* (1980-1983).

Alan Thicke would replace Alan Hamel and within a few years Canadian comedian Don Harron would take over the duties of talk show host as *The Don Harron Show* (1983-1985).

Don Harron is best known for the character Charlie Farquharson a personality that he portrayed on the CBS country music variety television show *Hee Haw.*

Don Harron passed away due to cancer in 2015.

Canadian Alan Thicke is a writer, singer, songwriter game show and talk show host and producer.

Alan Thicke was host of the CFCF 12 game show *First Impressions* (1976-1977) filmed in Montreal. He also produced CTV's music variety show *The Bobby Vinton Show* (1975-1978).

Alan Thicke was one of the script writers and producers for *Ferwood 2 Night* (1977) revamped as *America 2 Night* (1978) a spinoff of the soap opera parody *Mary Hartman, Mary Hartman.* (1976-1977).

He would host a CTV daily talk show *The Alan Thicke Show* (1980-1983) replacing the departing Alan Hamel in his time-slot.

Alan Thicke also wrote the television theme songs to the NBC sitcoms *Different Strokes* (1978-1985) and its spin-off *The Facts of Life* (1979-1988).

Alan Thicke would leave his CTV daily talk show for a syndicated late-night talk show, *Thicke of the Night* (1983-1984). *Thicke of the Night* was unable to compete with its talk show rival *The Tonight Show* starring Johnny Carson.

Once *Thicke of the Night* was cancelled, Alan Thicke would star in the popular ABC sitcom *Growing Pains* (1985-1992). In 2013, Alan Thicke was inducted into Canada's Walk of Fame.

My mother also enjoyed magazine style television shows such as; *McGowan & Co, McGowan's Montreal, McGowan's World* hosted by Montreal's favourite television weatherman Don McGowan and *Travel, Travel,* also hosted by Don McGowan and Montreal's favourite weatherwoman Suzanne Desautels.

These television programs were all produced in Montreal and aired on CFCF 12.

*****

Before Cable or Satellite Television was made readily available in Montreal, the Quebec household made due with a choice of four television stations (or channels).

Two English language stations, CBC Television affiliate CBMT Channel 6 and CTV Television Network affiliate CFCF Channel 12, and two French language stations, CBC Television affiliate CBFT Channel 2 and TVA Television affiliate CFTM Channel 10.

Locally produced programming, (although perhaps low budget, maybe poorly written, and lacking in production values), was abundant, very entertaining, fun and a joy to watch.

Author's Note:

I have heard and read the repeated confirmed and unconfirmed rumours, that sadly and unfortunately these important, historical television series and local programming were not saved, preserved, stored or archived.

Most of these television shows and series were recorded, broadcast and then taped over or destroyed.

Such a shame!

*****

While my mother enjoyed watching her favourite talk, magazine and game shows, I had my own documentary/games shows that I enjoyed watching.

👍☺ *Untamed World (1968-1976)* was narrated by Alan Small and featured documentaries on wildlife and primitive cultures.

👍☺ *Front Page Challenge* (1957-1995) was produced by CBC Television and aired on CBMT Channel 6.

While not necessarily a 'game show' *Front Page Challenge* was more of a 'game interview' program, where a panel of Canadian journalists would guess a news story and then interview the mystery guest associated with the news story.

Fred Davis was the host/moderator.

👍☺ *Reach for the Top* (1966-1985)

Also produced by CBC Television and aired on CBMT Channel 6.

Reach for the Top was an academic quiz show where teams of top high school students compete.

From 1966-1973 Canadian Alex Trebek was the host/ quizmaster.

👍☺ *Headline Hunters* (1972-1983) was produced by the CTV Television Network and aired on CFCF 12.

Headline Hunters was a game show where contestants were to identify a news event or newsmaker from clues given in the form of a headline.

Headline Hunters was hosted by Jim Perry.

Jim Perry would host *Headline Hunters* concurrently while hosting the game show *Definition*.

👍☺ *Definition* (1974-1989) Also produced by the CTV Television Network and airing on CFCF 12.

Definition was a word game where two teams of two contestants and celebrities would guess letters from a phrase of which the host had given a pun as a clue.

👆☺ *Know Your Sports* (1974-1978) Hosted by CFCF 12 sportscaster and CBC's *Hockey Night in Canada* broadcaster Dick Irvin. *Know Your Sports* was produced in Montreal and televised on CFCF 12.

A panel of three contestants would try to answer correctly a series of sports questions. *Know Your Sports* would become *Celebrity Know Your Sports* in its final season.

Author's Note:

I would 'whack my brain' to figure out the clues of each of these games shows but most often, end up guessing (some or most of) the answers.

*****

Recollections, events, brief histories & trivia:

👆☺ I bought my very first camera, a Kodak Pocket Instamatic (110-format).

The *Kodak Pocket Instamatic* was not complicated to use and it conveniently fit in my pants pocket, shirt pocket, and coat pocket.

I would bring the film cartridge to be developed at my neighbourhood photo processing store *Direct Film*.

Direct Film sold photographic film, assorted cameras and accessories, picture frames, photo albums and eventually VHS Video Tapes.

👆☺ On many occasions I shopped and purchased gifts at *Consumers Distributing* (French: *Distribution aux Consommateurs*), a catalogue/warehouse style store.

I would complete a product identification form from a merchandise catalogue, and patiently wait as the stock staff rummaged through warehouse inventory.

👆☺ Watching the CBC produced Keith Hampshire's *Music Machine* (1974-1976) a half hour music variety show on CBMT Channel 6.

Also appearing on the *Music Machine* was the six member vocal group Liberation (Roy Kenner, Lisa Dal Bello, Wayne St. John, Stephanie Taylor, Bill Ledster and Shawne Jackson).

The *Music Machine's* musical director was Doug Riley featuring his band Dr. Music.

Music Machine host Keith Hampshire was a popular Canadian singer known for the Canadian hit records 'Daytime-Night-time' (1972) and 'The First Cut Is the Deepest' (1973).

Keith Hampshire provided lead vocals for The Bat Boys release 'OK Blue Jays' (1983), which would become an anthem for Major League Baseball's Toronto Blue Jays. Blue Jays fans would sing the song/anthem during the seventh inning stretch of home games.

****

Dr. Music was a jazz/gospel group founded by Doug Riley. Their self-titled album contained the songs 'Sun Goes By' and 'One More Mountain to Climb'. Both songs would become Canadian classics.

Former Dr. Music band members Brian Russell and Brenda Gordon (who married and later divorced) would release (as Brian & Brenda) the album *Word Called Love* with the hits 'Gonna Do My Best to Love You' (1976), 'That's All Right Too' (1977).

Brenda Russell would release the solo hits 'So Good, So Right' (1979), 'Get Here' (1988) and 'Piano in the Dark' (1988).

*****

Roy Kenner joined guitarist Domenic Troiano's band Mandala and recorded the minor Canadian hit 'Love-it is' (1968). Mandala would break-up and become Bush. Bush's 'I Can Hear You Calling' (1970) and 'Young Street Patty' (1970) from their self-titled album would become minor hits.

Roy Kenner and Domenic Troiano would join the James Gang and release two albums *Straight Shooter* (1972) and *Passin' Thru* (1972). The song 'Run Run Run' (1972) was a minor hit. In 1973, Domenic Troiano would leave the James Gang to join The Guess Who, where he co-wrote with vocalist Burton Cummings, the Canadian hits 'Dancin' Fool' (1975) and 'Rosanne' (1975).

In 1979, Roy Kenner would provide vocals to Domenic Troiano's third solo album, *Fret Fever*. The singles 'We All Need Love' (1979) and 'It's You' (1979) would be huge hits in Canada.

In 1985, Domenic Troiano penned the television theme song of CTV's police drama series 'Night Heat' (1985-1991) with vocals by Roy Kenner.

*****

Shawne Jackson recorded the huge Canadian hit 'Just as Bad as You' (1974) which was written and produced by her husband Domenic Troiano.

Domenic Troiano passed away from prostate cancer in 2005.

*****

Lisa Dal Bello released her self-titled debut album produced by Canadian David Foster. The singles 'My Mind's Made Up' (1977) and 'Don't Wanna To Stand In Your Way' were minor hits.

She released the successful album *Pretty Girls* with the singles 'Pretty Girls' (1978) and 'Still In Love' (1978), both were huge hits in Canada.

Boz Scaggs released 'Miss Sun' (1980) with guest vocals by Lisa Dal Bello.

The album *Drastic Measures* (1981) was released, along with three minor hit singles 'Never Get To Heaven', 'Just Like You' and 'She Wants To Know'.

Lisa Dal Bello would take time off from recording to re-invent herself as Dalbello, and transform herself into an edgy rock singer.

Author's Note:

My brother George bought me a concert ticket and we went and saw Lisa Dal Bello perform live as the opening act for Burton Cummings on June 28, 1979 at the Montreal Forum.

✍☺ Also on CBMT Channel 6 the *King of Kensington* (1975-1980) was a great half hour sitcom, set in Toronto's Kensington

Market, about convenience store owner Larry King and his daily interactions with friends and neighbours.

The *King of Kensington* starred Al Waxman and Fiona Reid.

> Al Waxman was born in Toronto, Ontario. Al Waxman starred as Larry King on the CBC Television Network sitcom *The King of Kensington* (1975-1980).
>
> Al Waxman also starred as Lt. Bert Samuels on the CBS police drama *Cagney & Lacey* (1981-1988) starring Tyne Daley and Sharon Gless.
>
> He won a Gemini Award for his performance in the CBC Television Network film *Networth* (1995).
>
> In 1996, Al Waxman was inducted into the Order of Ontario and in 1997 was inducted into the Order of Canada.
>
> Al Waxman passed away during heart surgery in 2001. A statue of Al Waxman was erected in the Toronto neighbourhood, Kensington Market where his sitcom the *King of Kensington* took place.

♪♫ The exciting instrumental '*Cocktail*' (1975) by Montreal progressive band Morse Code is receiving much airplay on Montreal radio stations.

👍☺ I use to watch on CBMT Channel 6, the hour long police drama *Sidestreet* (1975-1978).

Sidestreet, (starred Sean McCann and Stephen Markle who were later replaced in the second season by Donnelly Rhodes and Jonathan Welsh) was a different type of police drama (set in the city of Toronto) which dealt with social issues instead of major crimes.

Jazz musician Chuck Mangione composed the *'Sidestreet Theme'* which can be found on the album *Feels So Good.*

Donnelly Rhodes was born in Winnipeg, Manitoba in 1937. He enrolled in Montreal's prestigious National Theatre School of Canada (French: École Nationale de Théâtre du Canada) which opened in 1960.

The National Theatre School of Canada located on rue St. Denis in Montreal is one of the most prestigious theatre schools in Canada, offering in English and French languages, courses or programs in acting, directing, playwriting, design and theatre production.

In 1974, Donnelly Rhodes joined the cast of the CBS soap opera *The Young and the Restless* (1974-1975). He returned to Canada for a starring role in the CBC police drama series *Sidestreet* (1976-1978). Donnelly Rhodes has guest starred in numerous American and Canadian television shows.

Donnelly Rhodes starred as Dutch Leitner in the ABC sitcom *Soap* (1978-1981).

Donnelly Rhodes later starred as marine veterinarian Grant "Doc" Roberts in the popular CBC adventure series *Danger Bay* (1985-1990) and he also played Detective Leo Shannon in the CBC dramatic series *Da Vinci's Inquest* (1998-2005).

🎵😊 *The Bobby Vinton Show* (1975-1978) was a half-hour weekly musical variety series, produced in Toronto by the CTV Television Network and aired on CFCF 12.

Bobby Vinton recorded many hit records during the 1960's; 'Blue on Blue' (1963), 'Roses Are Red' (1962) and 'Mr. Lonely' (1964).

With the success of the hit 'My Melody of Love' (1974), sung partially in English and Polish, Bobby Vinton would become known as the Polish Prince.

'My Melody of Love' (1974) would be used as the theme song to his show. *The Bobby Vinton Show* was so popular that it spawned a soundtrack album.

👍😑 October/November 1975, Montréal-Mirabel International Airport opens for business.

Due to the city of Montreal's international status Montréal-Mirabel International Airport (then the largest airport in the world) was designed and built to replace Dorval airport.

Under the Liberal Federal Government of Pierre Elliott Trudeau the Montréal-Mirabel International Airport opened in late 1975 in time for the 1976 Summer Olympics.

At that time it was decided that domestic and US flights would continue to be served by Dorval Airport while international flights would be served by Mirabel Airport.

For years International flights were scheduled out of Mirabel which was 50 minutes away from the downtown core while Dorval Airport was 20 minutes away. Travelers soon fell out of favour with Mirabel Airport (becoming a 'white elephant') as passengers had to take long bus rides or pay costly Taxi rides for connections from domestic to international flights while Montrealers had to travel far out of town for international flights.

In later years Mirabel Airport served as a cargo airport and an airplane testing site and has been deemed too out dated to be maintained.

Ironically Dorval Airport (underwent an expansion from 2000-2005) was renamed Pierre Elliott Trudeau Airport in 2004.

🎵👍🎵 The catchy 'Every Bit of Love' by Ken Tobias (1975) is climbing the Canadian music charts.

Canadian singer/songwriter Ken Tobias was born in Saint John, New Brunswick. He wrote the international hit 'Stay Awhile' (1970) recorded by Montreal band The Bells.

As a solo artist he released a string of hits including 'Dream #2' (1972), 'I Just Want to Make Music' (1973) 'Fly Me High' (1973) 'Run Away With Me' (1975) 'Give A Little Love' (1976) 'Dancer' (1977).

👍☺ I attended a screening of the filmed in Montreal, *Parasite Murders* (*Shivers* 1975) written and directed by Canadian David Cronenberg at the Atwater Cinema 2.

The Parasite Murders is a horror film starring Paul Hampton. A scientist is conducting experiments with parasites to be used in transplants, however once implanted the parasite causes an uncontrollable sexual desire in the host.

🎵👍🎵 Montreal's Suzanne Stevens tops the charts with 'Make Me Your Baby' (1975).

👍☺ 1975/76 season, the Montreal Canadiens beat the Philadelphia Flyers (in a best of seven games series 4 games to 0) to win their 19th Stanley Cup.

This would be the second Stanley Cup win for Montreal's head coach Scotty Bowman and the first in four consecutive Stanley Cup wins.

Scotty Bowman was born in Verdun, a borough of the City of Montreal. He began his professional coaching career as an assistant coach (and soon became the head coach replacing Lynn Patrick) when he joined the expansion St. Louis Blues. He coached The St. Louis Blues from 1967-1971 before joining the Montreal Canadiens in 1971.

Scotty Bowman coached the Montreal Canadiens from 1971-1979 winning the National Hockey League's Stanley Cup during the 1972-1973 season and winning four consecutive Stanley Cups from 1975-1979.

During the 1979-1980 seasons he joined the Buffalo Sabres as its General Manager and also doubled (off and on) as the team's coach until 1987. He then became a hockey analyst for CBC's Hockey Night in Canada.

He coached the Pittsburgh Penguins from 1991-1993 winning the Stanley Cup during the 1991-1992 season.

He coached the Detroit Red Wings from 1993-2002 until his retirement as coach, winning three Stanley Cups in 1996-1997, 1997-1998 and 2001-2002.

Scotty Bowman is the winningest coach in National Hockey League history.

In 2003, Scotty Bowman was inducted into Canada's Walk of Fame.

👎☹️👎 Appearing in their seventh Grey Cup the Montreal Alouettes were defeated at McMahon Stadium in Calgary by the Edmonton Eskimos 9-8.

👍☺️ I also purchased my first double edged safety razor and shaving cream

shaving episode

I recall one evening I was doing homework or studying for an exam, my concentration was disturbed by the sound of running water from the tap in the washroom. I didn't really think anything about it until I realized that the tap had been running water for quite some time. I got up from the kitchen table and walked down the hallway to investigate.

My bother George was there with what appeared to be white foam on the lower part of his face and in his hand was a razor.

I inquired what he was doing and he responded that he was in the process of shaving. George explained that shaving was the removal of facial hair with a razor, and that he had to be extremely careful while gliding the blade across his face so that he would not cut himself.

Intrigued, I stood and watched as George continued to shave his face. I asked George where he learned to shave and he explained that he had seen commercial advertising on television. I remember feeling my own face with the palm of my hand and thinking perhaps I should shave as well.

I began to pay closer attention to the commercials promoting men's shaving accessories that aired on television. Perhaps a month later, I attempted my first shave. Although I did not have heavy or thick facial stubble (or a five o'clock shadow) I was able to feel a small growth of fine hairs on my face, or what is commonly known as 'Peach Fuzz'.

At my local pharmacy establishment, I inquired about shaving creams and double-edged safety razors. In private and in a hushed tone I explained to the older male Pharmacist that my father had passed away when I was young and asked if he could explain the basics of shaving with a double edged razor.

Feeling confident (with myself) I purchased one of each item, and rushed home to experience my first shave.

Lathering my face was easy enough.

"Oh!" I whispered to myself as I gently glided the safety razor down my left cheek to the bottom of my jaw. "Aww…" I whispered a little louder as I completed shaving the left side of my face and began to shave the right side.

"Ouch!" I spoke out loud as I was shaving under my chin and down my throat.

"Shaving hurts!" I thought to myself, as I looked at my facial appearance in the mirror (that was attached to the washroom medicine cabinet).

"What the hell!" I exclaimed as I first noticed little spots of
blood in the reflection of the mirror. I had (what appeared to be)
a few small 'nicks and cuts' on my face. No doubt caused by and
inflected by the so-called 'safety razor'.

I rinsed my face with warm water, removing what shaving cream
that was left. I also applied five little pieces of torn toilet-paper to
the 'nicks and cuts' on my face.

A few moments later I gently removed the five pieces of torn toilet
paper and was about to apply a sample of my brother's aftershave
to my face.

Huge mistake…!

Removing the cover from the bottle, I sniffed the liquid contents. It
had a nice scent. I sprinkled some of the aftershave into my left hand.
I then mixed both my hands together and slowly began face tapping
both my cheeks, my chin and my throat (spreading the aftershave and
rubbing it evenly across the pores of my nicked and cut face).

Again, huge mistake…!

"Yaaaaooooooow…" I screamed.

I had never, ever, experienced a tingling, irritating, stinging,
burning face on fire sensation like that before. Taking a deep
breath and mustering all my courage, I continued to apply and rub
the aftershave to my face. "Ouch, Ouch, Ouch…"

*****

Because of the so-called 'Shaving Episode', (I am reminded of the old adage: *No shave, no pain*) I was really determined to find and purchase an aftershave or cologne that would not cause such a high degree of skin irritation.

Upon the advice and recommendations, of friends and relatives and in some instances, strangers, I purchased many different brand name colognes and aftershaves, to no avail!

One evening while studying for an exam, (my mother was watching television in the living room) I heard a woman's voice singing a catchy little jiggle *"There's something about an Aqua Velva man"*, curious as I was, I walked to the living room and questioned my mother about the commercial. She explained that it was a television advertisement for men's aftershave.

For one reason or another, that catchy little jingle stayed with me. I found myself humming it. Curious indeed!

Back to my local pharmacy establishment, where I found a few bottles of Aqua Velva Ice Blue in the men's grooming products aisle. I opened the bottle, sniffed the liquid contents and fell in love!

I questioned the pharmacist; he explained briefly, that Aqua Velva had been on store shelves since the early 1900's, and was introduced and distributed by the JB Williams Company.

Back home I shaved then splashed some Aqua Velva on my face. It felt so good, so invigorating and dare I say it…so manly! I would wear the aftershave with stubble on my face or clean shaved. Aqua Velva does cool, soothe and refreshes a man's face.

At school I received many compliments about the fragrance I was wearing. Walking to and from classroom to classroom, I could hear the whispers from many of my fellow female classmates. "David smells so good. Does anyone know what cologne he is wearing?"

I couldn't help but smile and hum to myself, *"There's something about an Aqua Velva man."*

Episode Epilog:

Through the years I have heard the comments that Aqua Velva aftershave is what is worn by the older gentleman. I have tried other brand name aftershaves, and I have always come back to wearing Aqua Velva for its soothing, cooling and refreshing sensation.

I am also a firm believer in the adage: *Once old is new again*

Do I still wear Aqua Velva Ice Blue?

Yes and no.

Aqua Velva Ice Blue has been repackaged and is now called Classic Ice Blue.

Other William's brand Aqua Velva aftershaves I have purchased, and would recommend; Aqua Velva Ice Sport Aqua Velva Musk and Aqua Velva Original Sport (apparently only sold in Canada).

Aqua Velva is now marketed by Combe Incorporated.

Do I consider myself to be an Aqua Velva man?

Yes I do!

"There's something about an Aqua Velva man".

Indeed there is...Indeed there is.

chapter eight

During the early to mid-seventies a new sound, a new genre of music was beginning to sweep the nation and the city of Montreal was no exception. The population of Quebec and Montreal embraced this sound and would become a pioneer in its love of, creation of and promotion of disco music.

The term disco was derived from the French word discothèque and subsequently evolved into an alternative word for 'nightclub'. Disco contains musical rhythms and musical elements of soul, pop, salsa and funk.

Disco music would become a worldwide phenomenon and the city of Montreal would become a major center of disco, second only to New York City in popularity as the place to be.

Montreal had its fair share of thriving discothèques during the disco craze, *1234*, *Club Rendezvous*, *Thursday's*, *Studio 55* and the *Limelight* (by far the most well-known Montreal discothèque).

The disco era in Montreal was not only about the music.

The disco era was also about strobe lights flashing, disco balls spinning, and popular dances such as the 'Robot', the 'Hustle' and the 'Bump'.

Men's fashion played its role as well; afro's, leisure suits were the clothes to wear, 'mood rings' and gold neck chains were the perfect accessories. A popular style of denim wear were the bell bottom jeans, flannel shirts, baseball jackets, headbands, flip-flop shoes, platform shoes and earth shoes.

Women's fashion included the perming of hair, wrap dress, tube tops, dresses with long thigh slits, and spandex short shorts along with kitten shoes and knee high boots.

Shag carpets, waterbeds and lava lamps were also the rage.

There was also a thriving drug scene happening in Montreal discothèques, especially for drugs that would enhance the experience of dancing to loud disco music and flashing lights. The drugs of choice were Quaaludes and cocaine.

Also during the disco era there was much promiscuity (the practice of having casual sex with different partners), orgies (group sex with multiple partners) and public sex in clubs and 'quickies' in alleyways.

The disco era in Montreal was first and foremost about the music; home-grown Montreal (French and English) talent produced and released some classic music during this time period.

- Suzanne Stevens - Make Me Your Baby (1975)
- André Gagnon - Wow (1975)
- Gloria Spring - Baby Come On (1976)
- Martin Stevens - J'aime La Musique (Comme Un Fou) (1976)

- Patsy Gallant - Are You Ready For Love/Libre Pour L'amour (1976)
- André Gagnon - Surprise (1976)
- Patsy Gallant - Sugar Daddy (1976)
- Toulouse - C'est Toujours A Recommencer/It Always Happens This Way(1976)
- Geraldine Hunt – J'ai Mal (1976)
- Boule Noire – Loin D'ici (1976)
- Martin Stevens - Love Is In The Air (1977)
- Pierre Perpall - J'aime Danser Avec Toi (1978)
- Alma Faye Brooks – If You Love Me Like You Say You Love Me (1977)
- Patsy Gallant - Stay Awhile/Aime-Moi (1977)
- Alma Faye Brooks - Stop, I Don't Need No Sympathy (1977)
- Toulouse – A.P.B. (1977)
- Montreal Sound – Music (1977)
- Patrick Norman with Black Light Orchestra – Let's Try Once Again (1977)
- Toulouse - What Would My Mama Say (1977)
- Patrick Norman - Sweet Sweet Lady (1978)
- Tony Green – Amoureux (1978)
- Boule Noire - Aimer D'Amour/Easy To Love (1978)
- Gino Soccio - Dancer (1979)
- France Joli - Come To Me (1979)
- Nightlife Unlimited – Love Is In You (1979)
- Freddie James - Get Up And Boogie (1979)
- Bombers – Get Dancin' (1979)

The rest of Canada was also dancing and moving to the disco beat and releasing huge dance hits.

- Brian & Brenda – Gonna Do My Best To Love You (1976)
- Claudja Barry – Dancin' Fever (1977)
- The Raes – Que Sera Sera (1977)
- Claudja Barry – Johnny Johnny Please Come Home (1977)
- The Raes – A Little Lovin' (Keeps The Doctor Away) (1978)
- Claudja Barry – Boogie Woogie Dancin' Shoes (1978)
- The Raes – I Only Wanna Get Up And Dance (1979)

chapter nine

In 1970 the city of Montreal was awarded the rights (by the International Olympics Committee) to host the 1976 Summer Olympic Games. French architect Roger Taillibert was commissioned by Montreal mayor Jean Drapeau to design a sports complex for the 1976 Summer Olympic Games.

Also in 1970, with the awarding of the 1976 Summer Olympic Games to the city of Montreal, construction began on the extension of the Montreal Metro System. To service the main Olympic site, Line 1 (Green Line) was extended from Frontenac to Honoré-Beaugrand.

The Olympic Stadium was built as the main venue and as a multi-purpose stadium for the 1976 Summer Olympic Games. It is nicknamed the 'the Big O' (in reference to its name) and also nicknamed 'the Big Owe' (for the astronomical cost).

Marred with controversy, cost overruns, scandals, construction delays and strikes, forced the Quebec Liberal government of Robert Bourassa to take over and oversee the project.

The 1976 Summer Olympic Games opened to an estimated attendance of 73,000 and an unfinished stadium.

Perceived and dubbed by many to be a white elephant (a possession which cannot be disposed of and/or its cost are out of proportion to its usefulness). In order to increase revenue to fund the rising costs of constructing the Olympic Stadium; the Quebec government applied a tobacco tax, and in 2006 the Olympic Stadium was paid off in full.

A few highlights from the 1976 Summer Games include:

- Nadia Comaneci, a Romania gymnast (14years old) would perform seven perfect scores, winning three gold medals.
- Russian strongman Vasiliy Alekseyev won a gold medal for weightlifting.
- Bruce Jenner a U.S. track and field athlete won the gold medal in the decathlon.
- Leon Spinks (*Light heavyweight*), his brother Michael Spinks (*Middleweight*) and Sugar Ray Leonard (*Light Welterweight*) each won gold medals for boxing while John Tate (*Heavyweight*) captured the bronze medal.

All four boxers would go on to win Professional Boxing Titles in their respected weight-class.
Canada as the host nation for the 1976 Summer Olympic Games, won 5 silver medals and six bronze medals.

Long time Montreal city councilor Nick Auf der Maur, was highly critical of Mayor Jean Drapeau.

Nick Auf de Maur was a journalist, columnist, politician and 'man about town' in Montreal. He wrote regular columns for The Montreal Star, The Montreal Gazette and the short lived Montreal Daily News.

As a politician, with frequent changes in political affiliations he was first elected to city council in 1974. He ran as a candidate in the 1976 provincial election and as a candidate during the 1984 federal election. He remained a city councilor until being defeated in 1994.

Nick Auf der Maur wrote the exposé book *The Billion-Dollar Game: Jean Drapeau and the 1976 Olympics* (1976) and co-authored with Robert Chodos and Rae Murphy, *Brian Mulroney: The Boy from Baie Comeau* (1984). *Nick: A Montreal Life* (1998) is a collection of his newspaper columns.

His daughter, the subject of many of his newspaper columns is photographer, musician, Melissa Auf der Maur.

A cigarette smoker and often seen at various Crescent Street bars including Winnie's Bar in downtown Montreal, fedoras wearing Nick Auf der Maur was not only a 'man about town' but 'a man of the people'…Montreal people.

Nick Auf der Maur passed away from cancer in 1998.

As a city councilor Nick Auf der Maur strongly opposed the renaming of Montreal streets, so in Nick's honor there is an alley way off of Crescent Street named Ruelle Nick Auf der Maur.

Canadian author Jack Ludwig wrote the insightful book *Five Ring Circus: The Montreal Olympics* (1976).

*****

Michael Douglas and Susan Anspach starred in the sports/drama film *Running* (1979) written and directed by Canadian Steven Hilliard Stern.

Michael Douglas stars as Michael Andropolis, a troubled American marathon runner and Olympic hopeful. The film deals with Michael's struggles of being unemployed and how he copes with a broken marriage.

Michael Andropolis is eventually chosen to participate in the 1976 Montreal Olympics.

Running was filmed partly in Montreal.

Academy Award winner (*Wall Street* 1987) Michael Douglas was nominated for a Genie Award for Best Performance by a Foreign Actor.

*****

The Olympic Stadium would become the home park for the following sport franchises;

- Canadian Football League's *Montreal Allouettes* (1976-1986, 1996-1997)
- National League Baseball's *Montreal Expo's* (1977-2004)
- North American Soccer League's *Montreal Manic* (1981-1983)
- World League of American Football's *Montreal Machine* (1991-1992).

The Olympic Stadium would also play host too many concerts such as Emerson, Lake and Palmer, AC/DC and Pink Floyd.

Emerson, Lake and Palmer would release the live album *Emerson, Lake and Palmer in Concert* (1979) recorded at an August 1977 show at the Montreal Olympic Stadium, which is featured on the album.

Recollections, events, brief histories & trivia:

♪♫♪ Married Canadian singing due Brian and Brenda (Russell) are topping the charts with 'Gonna Do My Best To Love You' (1976) written by Brian and Brenda Russell and David Foster.

✍☺ I recall channel surfing one evening (switching back and forth between two English television stations CTV and CBC) and decided to watch *Stars On Ice* (1976-1981).

Stars On Ice was a half-hour ice/variety show, produced in Toronto by the CTV Television Network and aired on CFCF Channel 12.

Stars On Ice featured Canadian and international skaters performing in multi-skater chorus lines or as solo performers.

Canadian Alex Trebek was the skating host and years later would be replaced by Doug Crosley in 1980.

Canadian Alex Trebek was born in Sudbury, Ontario in 1940. He began his broadcasting career for the CBC Television Network. Alex hosted *Music Hop* (1963-1964) a daily half-hour music show and was a host/quizmaster of the weekly half-hour, high school quiz show *Reach for the Top* (1966-1973)

During the nineteen seventies Alex Trebek hosted many American game shows; *The Wizard of Odds* (1973-1974), *High Rollers* (1974-1976 and 1978-1980), *Double Dare* (1976-1977).

He was also the ice skating host of the popular *Stars on Ice* produced by the CTV Television Network.

In 1984, he became internationally known as the host of the hugely successful *Jeopardy!*

In 2006, Alex Trebek was inducted to Canada's Walk of Fame.

🎵👍🎶 'Are You Ready For Love' (1976) by Patsy Gallant is a huge hit across Canada.

👍☺ The Montreal Expo's would play their final season of baseball (1976) at Parc Jarry.

👍☺ Watching the *Wolfman Jack Show* (1976-1977) a half hour music variety show hosted by radio personality Wolfman Jack.

The *Wolfman Jack Show* was produced in Vancouver by CBC Television and aired on CBMT Channel 6 in Montreal. The show featured the comedy of Montrealer's Peter Cullen and Danny Wells.

Wolfman Jack lent his voice to two Canadian songs 'Clap for the Wolfman' (1974) recorded by the Guess Who and 'Hit the Road, Jack' (1975) by The Stampeders.

Wolfman Jack passed away from a heart attack in 1995.

> Danny Wells was born in Montreal and made numerous guest appearances on television. Danny Wells appeared as a regular on the *Wolfman Jack Show* (1976-1977)
>
> Danny Wells is perhaps best known for his occasional role as 'Charlie' the bartender on the CBS comedy series *The Jeffersons*.
>
> Danny Wells was also a voice actor for television, film and videogames.
>
> Danny Wells passed away in 2013.

👍📖 I read the novel *The Main* (1976) by Trevanian a pen name of Rodney William Whitaker.

I had previously read Trevanian's *The Eiger Sanction* (1972), and was intrigued by the Montreal setting in *The Main*.

Police lieutenant Claude LaPointe is a streetwise veteran teamed with a by the book rookie to solve a murder.

🐌☺ *The David Steinberg Show* (1976-1977) was a Canadian half-hour comedy/variety show produced in Toronto by the CTV Television Network and aired on CFCF 12 in Montreal.

The David Steinberg Show (a TV show about a TV show) revolved around the behind the scenes adventures of the supporting cast, which included Joe Flaherty, John Canady, Dave Thomas and Martin Short.

The supporting cast would gain greater fame as the ensemble cast of SCTV.

Comedian David Steinberg was born in Winnipeg, Manitoba. In 1964, he joined The Second City in Chicago where he remained for a number of years. Stand-up comedian David Steinberg has made numerous guest appearances on television and has released many comedy albums.

During the 1976-1977 television seasons he was host of his own Canadian comedy/variety series *The David Steinberg Show* on the CTV Network.

David Steinberg has directed the feature films *Paternity* (1981) starring Burt Reynolds, *Going Berserk* (1983) starring John Candy and *The Wrong Guy* (1997) starring Dave Foley and Jennifer Tilly.

David Steinberg hosted the interview-style *Sit Down Comedy with David Steinberg* (2005-2007) show.
David Steinberg also wrote his first book titled *The Book of David* (2007).

In 2003, David Steinberg was inducted to Canada's Walk of Fame.

👍☺ Team Canada won the inaugural Canada Cup 1976 defeating Czechoslovakia in the final.

Following the success and public interest of the exciting 1972 and 1974 Summit Series where Canadian hockey players from both the National Hockey League (NHL) and the World Hockey Association (WHA) competed against the Soviet Union, there was a growing interest in an international ice hockey tournament.

Six teams competed in a best-of-five game round robin tournament (where each team meets all other teams in turn) concluding with a best-of-three game series final.

Setting aside the bitter rivalry between the NHL and WHA, the Canadian team selected players from both leagues.

The 1976 Canada Cup was held from September 2-15, 1976.

1976 Canada Cup Series:

- September 02, 1976: **Canada** 11 - Finland 2
- September 03, 1976: **Sweden** 5 - United States 2
- September 03, 1976: **Czechoslovakia** 5 - Soviet Union 3
- September 05, 1976: **Sweden** 3 – Soviet Union 3
- September 05, 1976: **Czechoslovakia 8** – Finland 0
- September 05, 1976: **Canada** 4 – United States 2
- September 07, 1976: **Soviet Union** 11 – Finland 3
- September 07, 1976: **Czechoslovakia** 4 – United States 4
- September 07, 1976: **Canada** 4 – Sweden 4
- September 09, 1976: **Finland** 8 – Sweden 6
- September 09, 1976: **Soviet Union** 5 – United States 0
- September 09, 1976: **Czechoslovakia** 1 – Canada 0
- September 11, 1976: **United States** 6 – Finland 3
- September 11, 1976: **Sweden** 2 - Czechoslovakia 1

- September 11, 1976: **Canada** 3 – Soviet Union 1

Canada Cup Final:

- September 13, 1976: **Canada** 6 – Czechoslovakia 0
- September 15, 1976: **Canada** 5 – Czechoslovakia 4

Team Canada won the 1976 Canada Cup Tournament.
Team Canada coaches included Scotty Bowman, Don Cherry,
Bobby Kromm and Al MacNeil.
Defenseman Bobby Orr was named Most Valuable Player.

Also from December 27, 1976 to January 8, 1977 the Soviet Red
Army toured North America to compete against hockey teams
from the WHA in a best-of eight game Super Series '76-'77. The
Red Army would win the tournament 6 games to 2.

Super Series '76-'77:

- December 27, 1976: **New England Whalers** 5 – Red Army 2
- December 28, 1976: **Red Army** 7 - Cincinnati Stingers 5
- December 30, 1976: **Red Army** 10 - Houston Aeros 1
- January 01, 1977: **Red Army** 5 - Indianapolis Racers 2
- January 03, 1977: **Red Army** 6 - San Diego Mariners 3
- January 05, 1977: **Red Army** 3 - Edmonton Oilers 2
- January 06, 1977: **Red Army** 3 - Winnipeg Jets 2
- January 08, 1977: **Quebec Nordiques** 6 – Red Army 1

chapter ten

1976, now that was a year for the city of Montreal.

The construction of and the opening of Montreal Mirabel Airport
(at that time the world's largest airport) in late 1975 was greeted by
mixed reviews and concerns.

It was decided to transfer International flights to Mirabel while
domestic and US flights continued to be served by Dorval airport.

During 1975/76 Stanley Cup Finals the Montreal Canadiens beat
the Philadelphia Flyers to win their 19th Stanley Cup.

The 1976 Montreal Summer Olympics was a huge success,
regardless of the cost, the numerous delays in construction and the
Olympic Stadium not being finished on time.

The opening ceremonies of the Montreal Summer Olympics drew
an attendance of 73,000 spectators.

The extension to Line 1 or the green line of the Montreal Metro
System was also a huge success with Montreal passengers and
tourists.

The economy was booming and the city of Montreal was on the international map. At that time Montreal was the biggest and richest city in Canada.

Team Canada defeated Czechoslovakia to win the 1976 Canada Cup Tournament.

Regardless of all the success and prosperity the city of Montreal enjoyed during 1976, the smell of change was in the air for the population and the province of Quebec.

Promising to provide good government and a referendum for political independence within its first mandate, on November 15, 1976, (Election Day in Quebec) René Lévesque's Parti Québécois defeated the Quebec Liberal government of Robert Bourassa.

On November 25, 1976 René Lévesque was sworn in as premier of Quebec.

As for me my last year of Junior High School or Secondary School was uneventful. My grades were good, not great but good. I was working part-time; I had money in my pocket. My sister and brother were both working full-time.

To help relieve (my mother) the burden of paying all the household bills by herself, we were all contributing monetarily to the household.

While some of my school friends were participating in after school activities (*The Chess Club, Cosom and/or Floor Hockey*), other friends were participating in another form of after school activity. The opposite sex...

Aside from a few spoken words and class assignments, the opposite sex had gone mostly unnoticed during my elementary school years.

Maturing (both mentally and physically) from boyhood to adolescent, I was becoming more and more aware of my surroundings and a part of my surroundings was the opposite sex.

Between attending secondary school, homework and working part-time twenty-five hours a week, my daily schedule was quite full. However, I was still able to spend time with classmates outside from school.

Quite often a few of us would ride the metro system to downtown Montreal. We would walk along St. Catherine Street, joking among ourselves, window shopping and sneaking looks and glances at the pretty women walking by. We tried to be as inconspicuous as we possibly could be. I wonder if we were.

Usually our journeys to the downtown core of Montreal would lead us to *Les Terraces.*

    Les Terraces (1976-1987) was an underground downtown mall, adjacent to Eaton's department store (now-defunct) and connected to the McGill metro station. *Les Terraces* housed over 100 stores and counter restaurants. The mall floors were color-coded and interconnected, allowing easy walking access to the top of the mall (street level).

David Makin

Extensive construction followed the closing of *Les Terraces* which was renamed the Montreal Eaton Center (Centre Eaton) and opened to the public in 1991.

Eaton's department store was a retail institution in Montreal and other major cities in Canada. The downtown Montreal based, nine story Eaton's store was located on St. Catherine Street. The Eaton's company folded in 1999.

Following a complete interior redesign, the downtown Eaton's store, opened to the public as the Complexe Les Ailes.

One Friday afterschool in April 1977, I was strolling through *Les Terraces* and met a friend from school. Marie and I had known each other since elementary school.

Although we had hardly spoken, we were friendly and courteous to one another. We would exchange nods, glances and salutations.

Marie explained that she was waiting to meet her mother; they had made arrangements to do some shopping. We decided that we would keep each other company until her mother arrived.

We walked around and up and down the floor levels of *Les Terraces,* looking in the store windows, talking and laughing. We discussed our school classes, homework, we gossiped about our fellow classmates and teachers. We spoke of our families.

I enjoyed very much that Friday afternoon with Marie. She was interesting, funny, easy to talk to and very attractive. Very attractive!

Recollections, events, brief histories & trivia:

👌☺ 1976/77 season, The Montreal Canadiens won their 20th Stanley Cup by defeating the Boston Bruins (in a best of seven game series 4-0).

This would be the third Stanley Cup win for Montreal's head coach Scotty Bowman and the second in four consecutive Stanley Cup wins.

👌☺ Also during the 1976/77 season, the Quebec Nordiques of the World Hockey Association (WHA) defeated the Winnipeg Jets to win the Avco World Trophy or Avco Cup.

👌☺ April 15, 1977, with an attendance of over 57,000, the Montreal Expos played their season opener and first baseball game at Montreal Olympic Stadium, losing to the Philadelphia Phillies 7-2.

♪👌♫ 'I'm A Fool' (1977) by Montreal singer/songwriter and record producer Tony Green is receiving a heavy rotation on Montreal radio stations.

chapter eleven

I thought about Marie that whole weekend and I couldn't wait to see her at school.

The following Monday, I awoke to the voice of 98 CKGM's Ralph Lockwood. I giggled to myself when he asked his listening audience *"How's your oiseau?"* (How's your bird?).

I showered and shaved, splashed on some *Aqua Velva Ice Blue,* dressed quickly and left for school earlier than I normally would.

Marie was already at school, chatting with friends when I arrived. I greeted my friends and fellow classmates; we discussed what we did on the week-end and slowly made our way to homeroom class.

Morning seemed to pass slowly as the lunch hour approached. Downstairs in the cafeteria, seated, I was unfolding and opening a brown paper bag that contained my lunch, a ham and cheddar cheese sandwich on sliced whole wheat bread, when I spotted Marie. She was also seated with friends.

I finished eating my ham and tomato sandwich, crumpled the brown paper bag and walked towards a waste container. I deposited the brown paper bag in the waste container and was heading towards the exit to the school yard, when I noticed Marie approaching.

"Hi Marie" I said and continued, "How are you? How was your week-end?"

She greeted me with a "Hello David. I'm okay, I guess." By her response and the tone of her voice, I could sense that all was not well with Marie.

"Would you like to talk about it?" I asked.

"No, not really." she responded in a low but firm tone. I didn't really know what to say.

"David, I'm sorry...I'm just not very happy today." She said with a touch of sadness. I may have been wrong but I am quite sure I had seen tears well up in her eyes. "It's okay...If you should need a friend to talk to, I am here for you." I said reassuringly.

She thanked me for my concern and I continued my way towards the school yard exit. I was no sooner outside when I heard Marie's voice behind me. "David...Wait up!" I stopped, turned to the direction of her voice and watched Marie as she walked towards me.

"Can I walk with you?" she asked. I quickly responded "Of course you can." Without speaking a word we slowly walked to the end of the school yard.

"We're moving..." she said softly.

"What do you mean?" I wasn't sure I heard her correctly.

"My family, they're thinking about moving." She clarified.

"You mean you're moving to another district..." I said.

"David, you don't understand!" Marie started to cry, "My father is thinking about moving to Toronto."

Marie was correct I did not understand. I was momentarily stunned by the news.

"What? Why?" I inquired.

Marie inhaled a deep breath of air and continued "The plant where my father works is closing down. One of the company bosses asked my father if he wanted to relocate to Toronto." Still confused I asked again "But why?

Why is the company closing?"

Marie opened her purse and extracted a couple of tissues, wiped her tearing eyes and continued, "It's the economy, and the new PQ government... even my Uncle Peter is thinking of moving out of Quebec.

November 1976, then Quebec Premier Robert Bourassa's provincial Liberal government were defeated by the Parti Québécois.

Due to language controversies (in 1974 the Liberal government of Robert Bourassa implemented the Official Language Act (Bill 22) which made French the sole official language of the province of Quebec. Bill 22 angered the Anglophone population while the Francophone population felt Bill 22 was not enough) and corruption scandals (due to construction delays and cost overruns stemming from the 1976 Montreal Summer Olympic Games) the Liberal government lost the 1976 provincial election.

The Parti Québécois is a separatist (*to advocate separation from a larger group*) provincial political party in Quebec. Led by a former journalist and a former Quebec Liberal Party cabinet minister, René Lévesque would become the 23rd Premier of Quebec.

Celebrated mostly, by the French speaking population, the 1976 Provincial election victory, future language laws and a 1980 Quebec referendum, would result in an economic downfall, business closures, company relocations and mass departures of the English speaking population.

"Do you know when you might be moving to Toronto?" I asked.

"Possibly as soon as this summer in July, right now it is only talk but my father is willing to move but my mom is not. My parents have been discussing it and sometime they have argued." whispered Marie.

"Oh boy..." I responded.

"I don't want to move, David. All my friends are here in Montreal!" Marie was now overcome with emotion; she extracted more tissues from her purse.

I am not really sure what my feelings were at that moment, but I knew I could feel Marie's pain. I moved in a little closer to her and put my right arm around her shoulders. I tried my best to console her.

"Don't cry, Marie. Everything will work out. You'll see." I whispered softly.

I let Marie regain her composure and then we slowing walked back towards school. As we approached the school entrance, I noticed some of my friends and some of Marie's friends sneaking looks and glances in our direction. My friend Joe nodded approvingly, and with his left hand gave me a 'thumbs up'.

I asked Marie "Are you going to be alright?" Marie looked at me, nodded affirmatively, and then she said "I should go and wash my face!" I agreed.

Marie then took a few steps forward, abruptly stopped, turned back and said "Thank you, David." I responded with a brave smile.

Emotional and unexpectedly she threw both her arms around my neck and shoulders and gave me a hug. I hugged her back. I reassured Marie of my friendship. She whispered "Thank you..." in my ear. She then kissed me on the cheek and made her way towards the school entrance.

I watched Marie as she entered the school; I reached into my right side pants pocket, pulled out a square cardboard paper package and extracted a cigarette from inside. I placed the cigarette between my lips, reached again into my pants pocket for a book of matches, lit the cigarette and slowly inhaled

Author's Note:

Marie and her family's story, would be an example of other countless similar stories to be heard, discussed and debated on radio, television, in bars, restaurants, coffee shops, street corners and households throughout Montreal, Quebec and Canada for years to come.

Due to the political climate in Quebec, more than handful of my friends and their families would leave the Province of Quebec and relocate to other Provinces and cities.

My sister Ellen with her boyfriend would also leave Montreal for Toronto and years later British Columbia.

cigarette episode

I woke up one morning with a sore throat. I went to school and later to work. Nick, one of my fellow co-workers in the kitchen noticed that I was 'clearing my throat' quite often and asked me if anything was wrong.

I explained that I had woken up with a sore throat and that the lozenges I purchased were soothing my throat, but only for a short period of time.

While we were on break, Nick offered me a cigarette. I thanked him and explained that I was a 'non-smoker'. Understanding, he went on to explain that he 'smoked' menthol cigarettes and that the menthol flavor would help soothe my sore throat.

There was no pressure to try one. If it helped soothe my sore throat, fine. If the menthol cigarette didn't help soothe my throat, well no harm done.

He opened his package of cigarettes and extended one to me. I accepted and thanked him as I placed the filtered end between my lips. Reaching into his pants pocket he extracted a book of matches and lit the tobacco end of the cigarette.

I inhaled the cigarette smoke in my mouth and quickly released it (into the atmosphere). The menthol cigarette really did have a menthol taste to it. I toke another 'puff', a small one, this time I slowly inhaled the menthol cigarette into my throat and lungs. I cannot begin to explain the feeling.

Most people who sample a cigarette for the first time would begin to cough. Some people would begin to feel sick, turn green and most probably vomit. I did not experience any of the above mentioned beginners symptoms. I was a first time professional smoker. No turning green, no acid reflux or vomiting and no coughing. The menthol cigarette smoke, actually did feel good as I inhaled it into my throat and lungs. It was both calming and soothing.

I soon learned that many of the small corner convenience stores would sell individual cigarettes for a dime. Others would sell cigarettes for a nickel. Needless to say I would purchase a few cigarettes every day. Eventually I was given the advice to buy a package of cigarettes instead of a few cigarettes at a time.

At first I would buy a pack of menthol cigarettes and eventually switched to smoking regular tobacco tasting cigarettes. I have tried both filtered and non-filtered cigarettes, but I preferred filtered cigarettes. I progressed from smoking a few 'cigs' a day, to smoking a half pack and eventually a full pack.

Slowly the public was informed and made aware of the dangers and hazards caused by smoking cigarettes.

Episode Epilog:

Back then smoking cigarettes was commonplace. Cigarette
smoking was visible everywhere, from television commercials,
to motion pictures, television series, newspaper and magazine
advertising.

   We could smoke at the workplace, in bars, restaurants, on city
buses, in taxi cabs and hospitals.

   Smokers could purchase individual packages and/or cartons
(8 pack per) of cigarettes practically anywhere; from cigarette
vending machines, grocery stores, convenience stores and
pharmacy establishments.

   If I had known or been informed earlier in my life or been
advised of the dangers and long term effects of smoking cigarettes,
I probably would not have started or continued smoking.

   Cigarette smoking and I would go on to share an on and off and
a love and hate relationship that would last some 35 years.

chapter twelve

I graduated Junior High School and in September I was starting
Senior High. I was still working at The Texan Restaurant. I was
promoted from dishwasher to short order cook or line cook.

Actually I was still working a few shifts as dishwasher and a
couple of shifts as a short order cook. Cooking at The Texan was
fun. The kitchen staff was very patient with me.

Starting me off slowly, in the salads and sandwiches section (and
eventually working the grill) the owner Mister George gave me a
raise in my hourly wage as well.

Marie and her family did not move to Toronto, although the
thought was not far from their minds. The plant where Marie's
father worked remained opened in Montreal (for the time being)
and her father was still employed. Marie's Uncle Peter would leave
the province of Quebec and move out west to Alberta.

Since that day that Marie confided in me that she and her family
were thinking about moving to Toronto, we became fast friends.

We both tried to not become too emotionally attached to each other but over time (it did not take too long) we both were developing feelings towards one another.

We were friends, not only friends but more than friends. Not dating, but spending time together. No strings attached but emotionally linked.

During the school summer vacation, Marie and I would 'hangout' together. I brought Marie to Belmont Park, an amusement park in the (then) Montreal neighbourhood of Cartierville. We spent the day at the amusement park, playing games and enjoying ourselves on the many rides.

My favourite ride was the *Cyclone* (a wooden roller coaster) while Marie preferred the 'haunted house' and the distorting mirror.

Belmont Park (1923-1983) was a popular amusement part in the (then) Montreal neighbourhood of Cartierville.

Belmont Park was privately owned and had at one time a Ferris wheel, a carousel and numerous other rides for children and adults. The *Cyclone* was by far the most popular ride and a favourite attraction for the park.

Belmont Park also had a picnic area, a swimming pool, a dance hall and a roller skating rink.

Belmont Park closed in October 1983.

Marie and I would also go window shopping downtown on rue Sainte-Catherine or I would buy us a bite to eat at a local fast food restaurant where we would insert quarters in the tableside 'jukebox' and play our favourite songs.

I recall Marie turning the knob and flipping through the song selector until she instructed me to insert a quarter and to press A3 on the 'jukebox' keypad. After a few brief moments Nanette Workman's 'The Queen' began to play.

Singer/songwriter Nanette Workman was born in Brooklyn, New York; she recorded the French song 'Et Maintentant' in 1966. The song was a huge hit in the province of Quebec. Nanette Workman also supplied back-up vocals to a few Rolling Stones songs such as 'Honky Tonk Woman'.

Nanette Workman recorded (in both French and English) and released a string of hit singles in Quebec including a French version of Patti Labelle's 'Lady Marmalade' (1975), followed by the French language hits 'Danser Danser' (1975), 'Donne Donne' (1976) and the English language hits 'Crying, Crying' (1976) and the hugely successful 'The Queen' (1976).

Nanette's bother is Billy Workman (a well-known session musician in Quebec) who released the moderate hit 'Talk About Money' (1977) which was produced by Quebec rocker Michel Paglario and George Lagios.

Nanette also lent her powerhouse vocals to Mahogany Rush's hit 'Sister Change' (1979) and Boule Noire's mega hit 'Aimer D'Amour' (1978) as well as the English version 'Easy To Love' (1978)

In 1999, Nanette released the biographical book (with photographs) Nanette.

Nanette Workman has continued to record music and make live appearances.

The 'jukebox' speakers were not the best but the song could be heard ever so squeaky.

The waitress appeared with pen and note pad in hand, we ordered a 'Club Sandwich' for two with a couple of sodas.

Marie once again instructed me to insert another quarter and to press H7 on the 'jukebox' keypad. I could hear the intro to Boule Noire's Quebec hit 'Loin D'Ici' (1977).

Boule Noire is George Thurston (1951-2007) who was raised in Saint-Jérôme, Quebec. Singer/songwriter George Thurston would work as a session musician for many well-known Quebec artists.

George Thurston released his debut album Boule Noire (1976) featuring the Quebec hits 'Aimes-Tu La Vie Comme Moi' (1976), 'Loin Loin De La Ville' (1976). He would also write songs for the female trio Toulouse who had sung back ground vocals on many of his and other artist's recordings.

Toulouse we're a trio of backing vocalists (Judi Richards, Heather Gauthier and Mary Lou Gauthier) who decided to form a group. Following the release of their self-titled debut album, Lorri Zimmerman replaced Mary Lou Gauthier. Their first hit single 'C'est Toujours A Recommencer' (1976) was released a year later in English as 'It Always Happens This Way' (1977) followed by 'A.P.B'. (1977) 'What Would My Mama Say (1977) and 'Don't Play With My Heart' (1978). Liette Lomez joined the group in 1979.

Sadly Liette Lomez passed away from cancer of the gallbladder in 2014.

George Thurston became a sensation in Quebec with the follow up hits 'Loin D'Ici' (1977) 'Constance' (1978) and the mega hit 'Aimer D'Amour' (1978) with power background vocals by Nanette Workman.

'Barbados Girl' (1979) 'Love Me Please Love Me' (1980) soon followed making George Thurston one of the prominent figures of dance and R&B music in Quebec.

The great bilingual 'I'd Like To Be With You My Baby (En Amour)' (1991) received airplay on both French and English radio in Montreal. 'Easy To Love' (1978) was the English version of 'Aimer D'Amour'.

In 2007, George Thurston released his autobiography titled after his hit single *Aime Tu La Vie?*

Sadly George Thurston passed away from colorectal cancer in 2007.

The waitress arrived with two half's of a Club Sandwich with two sodas. We thanked her and she wished us a 'Bon Appétit'.

I grabbed a French 'frie' from my plate and bit into it. It was nice and crispy and full of flavour. Marie had also taken a 'frie' from her plate and proceeded to dip the 'frie' in a small puddle of ketchup she had squirted from a bottle that was already placed on the table.

Marie asked me to insert another quarter and to press D5 on the 'jukebox' keypad. The intro to Richard Tate's 'Fill My Life With Love' (1977) could be heard from the 'jukebox' speakers.

Richard Tate was a Montreal session musician, who recorded in both English and French.

He co-wrote the hit 'Fill My Life With Love' (1977) which would recorded a year later by American disco group Saint Tropez.

Richard Tate also released the hit 'She's Got the Time to Love Me' (1977)

116

I had wished Marie (who was chewing a mouthful of toast, chicken, mayonnaise, lettuce, bacon and tomato) a 'Bon Appétit' just as she bit into a triangle of her Club Sandwich.

******

On another occasion I recall a late Saturday afternoon I was escorting Marie home when we noticed a hand printed sign advertising a 'garage sale'. I was curious and asked Marie if she wanted to take a quick look around the 'garage sale'.

We followed the directions on the hand printed sign and found that the 'garage sale' was really a 'backyard sale'

We entered the backyard and were greeted by the proprietors of the 'backyard sale' who cheerfully suggested we look around and "Buy, buy, buy." We thanked the proprietors and casually browsed from table to table.

There were five tables with cardboard boxes containing 'second hand' clothes, stacks of books, record albums and 45rpm's, and 8-track tapes.

Marie and I were more or less ready to leave when I noticed something leaning against one of the tables. It was a guitar. I had always (secretly) wanted to play guitar.

The guitar was not new. It was as it was advertised, a second hand, used, beaten up, scratched Gibson acoustic guitar. I bought it right away.

The 'backyard sale' proprietors informed me that included with the purchase of the guitar was a beginner's guide to playing guitar manual and a few guitar picks. Inside the manual were charts displaying finger positioning to form the guitar chords.

I was excited and ready to 'rock'!

******

I practiced the guitar as often as I could, sometimes late into the night. I can still hear my mother's voice, yelling from her room across the hall, telling me to "Put that darn guitar away and go to sleep. You're disturbing the neighbours." she would say. I guess she wanted to say that I was disturbing her and the household but she would use the neighbours as the excuse.

After a few short summer months of practice and numerous adhesive bandages for my sore, sometimes bleeding fingers, I was attempting to play some of my favourite songs.

One of the very first songs I learned to play on guitar was Michel Paglario's 'Rainshowers'.

Michel Pagliaro is a legend in the Quebec music industry, writing and recording in both French and English.

Michel Pagliaro released in French the songs; 'J'Entends Frapper' (1972), 'M'Lady' (1969), 'Fou De Toi' (1972).

The English hits 'Rainshowers' (1972) 'Lovin' You Ain't So Easy' (1971) and 'Some Sing Some Dance' (1972) were released from his self-titled debut English album (recorded at Abby Roads

Studio in London). 'What the Hell I Got' (1975) 'Timerace' (1977), would become instant classics on radio stations throughout Quebec.

Michel Pagliaro would retreat from the music business for many year before coming back full force with the great comeback hits 'Dangereux' (1988), 'Les Bombes' (1988) and 'L'espion' (1988) with the catchy one English line "All I want to do is to be with you" were huge hits in Quebec.

In 2008, Michel Pagliaro received the Governor General's Performing Arts Award for Lifetime Artistic Achievement.

Another song I learned to play on guitar was 'Sweet City Woman' (1971) by the Canadian rock trio The Stampeders.

The Stampeders are a Canadian band from Calgary, Alberta. Rich Dodson, Kim Berly and Ronnie King formed the rocking trio. 'Sweet City Woman' would become an international hit.

The Stampeders would release many classic Canadian singles; 'Carry Me' (1971), 'Wild Eyes' (1972) 'Oh My Lady' (1973) 'Running Wild' (1973) and a remake of 'Hit the Road Jack' (1975), featuring the voice of radio personality Wolfman Jack.

The Stampeders also released a French language version of 'Sweet City Woman' titled Oui Tu Est Mon Amie (1971).

I understood the basics of playing the guitar and I was able to form a few chords allowing me to play a few songs. I did not consider myself a guitar player.

Although I was self-taught, (perhaps not correctly self-taught) that however, did not stop me from attempting to write and compose an original song every so often.

Recollections, events, brief histories & trivia:

✍☺ I enjoyed watching the talented and beautiful Patsy Gallant perform on *The Patsy Gallant Show* (1977-1979) a weekly half hour variety show.

The Patsy Gallant Show was produced at CFCF 12 in Montreal.

Patsy Gallant was born in 1948 and is a native of New Brunswick. Her family moved to Montreal when she was ten.

Patsy Gallant released the minor hit 'Get That Ball' (1972) followed by the French 'Raconte' (1974) and the hit 'Makin' Love In My Mind' (1975).

In 1976 Patsy Gallant was dubbed as a disco diva upon the release of the hugely successful *Are You Ready For Love* (1976) album and the hits 'Sugar Daddy' (1976) and 'Are You Ready For Love' (1976).

1977 she released the *Will You Give Me Your Love* (1977) album and the hits 'Every Step of the Way' (1977) and 'Stay Awhile With Me' (1977) along with the French album *Besoin D'Amour* (1977) with the French hits 'Libre Pour L'Amour' (1977), and 'Besoin D'Amour' (1977).

Success continued with the release of the English album *Patsy!* and the French album *Patsy Gallant Et Star*. The hit 'O Michel' was released in both languages.

Patsy Gallant was married to and later divorced pianist, singer and composer Dwayne Ford.

*****

Dwayne Ford was born and raised in Edmonton, Alberta. As a member of Bearfoot, Dwayne Ford wrote the hits 'Molly' (1973) 'Passing Time' (1974) and 'There's A Life In Me' (1974).

After the break-up of Bearfoot, Dwayne Ford was in high demand as a session musician recording with Quebec rocker Michel Pagliaro and Patsy Gallant whom he married.

In 1981 Dwayne Ford released a solo album, the superb *Needless Freaking* that he co- produced with David Foster. The hit Lovin' and Losin' You (1981) was released from the *Needless Freaking* album.

*****

With the slowing decline of disco music Patsy Gallant retreated from the music industry and years later moved to Paris, France where she starred for eight years in Luc Plamondon's critically acclaimed *Starmania*.

👆😀 Watching the film *The Pyx* (1973) starring Karen Black, Canadian actor Christopher Plummer and Quebec actor Donald Pilon on CBMT channel 6's Saturday Night Movies (1977).

The Pyx was filmed in Montreal.

Two Montreal detectives investigate the death of a prostitute and uncover evidence that leads to a satanic cult. *The Pyx* was based on the novel by Montreal author John Buell.

John Buell (1927-2013) was born in Montreal and was a teacher at Montreal's Concordia University.

John Buell wrote the novels *The Pyx* (1959), *Four Days* (1962), *The Shrewsdale Exit* (1972), *Playground* (1976), and *A Lot To Make Up For (1990).*

The film *L'Agression* (1973), starring Catherine Deneuve and Jean-Louis Trintignant, was based on the John Buell novel *The Shrewsdale Exit.*

👍☺ *Feel Like Dancin'* (1977-1979) was a weekly one hour music show featuring musical acts lip-syncing their latest singles and young adults dancing to the latest dance hits.

Feel Like Dancin' was filmed at CFCF Studios and broadcast on CFCF 12 in Montreal. *Feel Like Dancin's* opening theme was the disco funk tune 'It Makes You Feel Like Dancin'' (1977) by Rose Royce.

Ian Finley was the host of *Feel Like Dancin'*.

Ian Finley performed voice work for many radio and television commercials and was also a week-end radio announcer at CJFM FM 96 in Montreal.

♫👍♫ Quebec singer Michel Stax released an incredible French interpretation of Paul Anka's 'Let Me Get To Know You' (1973) with 'Dites-Lui Que Je L'Aime' (1977).

♫👍♫ The disco song 'Baby Come On' (1976) by Gloria Spring is receiving much air-play a year after its release on Montreal radio stations. 'Baby Come On' was produced by Montrealer George Lagios.

> George Lagios was a Montreal musician, songwriter, record producer and a pioneer in the Quebec music industry. During the nineteen sixties George Lagios produced records for Quebec singer Renée Martel, and the popular Quebec group César et les Romains.
>
> George Lagios also produced legendary Quebec 'rocker' Michel Pagliaro in both languages including the French hits 'A T'aimer' (1970), 'Pour Toi, Pour Toi' (1970), 'Fou De Toi' (1972) and the English classics 'Lovin' You Ain't Easy' (1971), 'Rainshowers' (1971), 'Some Sing, Some Dance' (1971), 'What The Hell I Got' (1976).

George Lagios, and Michel Paglario produced Walter Rossi's self-titled debut album and George produced Walter Rossi's second album the fantastic *Six Strings Nine Lives* (1978) which featured the hits 'Slowdown, Slowdown' (1978) and 'Ride the Wind' (1978). Walter Rossi joined George Lagios' disco studio project Bombers playing guitar on two albums and the hit 'Keep on Dancin'' (1979).

Montreal actress/singer Celine Lomez was produced by George Lagios on the hit album *Burning* (1980) and released the hit singles 'Be Mine' (1980) and 'Winning' (1980).

In 1993, George co-produced the April Wine album *Attitude* with April Wine front man Myles Goodwyn and released the great comeback hit 'If You Believe In Me'.

Sadly George Lagios passed away in December 2014.

Author's Note:

It was during the recording of April Wine's *Atititude* (1993) album I had met George Lagios at Le Den in Westmount, Quebec (a little restaurant/bistro/coffee shop I owned for a couple of years).

I had the pleasure to discuss over countless cups of coffee with him the recordings and artists that he had worked with and produced.

I enjoyed the many conversations we had. George Lagios was honest, kind, intelligent and a warm human being.

chapter thirteen

One summer Tuesday afternoon I was finishing a work shift at the *Texan Restaurant*. The day was uneventful; I had started work at 8 am and was finished by 3 pm, during my work break I phoned Marie, she was finishing some house work but agreed to meet me after work. We decided to walk around and explore Old Montreal.

In 1642, a group of French settlers founded Montreal (known as Old Montreal).

Old Montreal still has a few remaining buildings dating back to the 17th Century. The architecture and many of the cobbled streets have been restored and maintained to resemble the look of the city during its days as a settlement. The guided horse drawn calèches also help to maintain the image of the settlement.

Old Montreal is the oldest area of the city of Montreal and is a favourite tourist attraction.

Marie had begun to complain about the uncomfortable pair of shoes she was wearing and how sore her feet were when we decided to call it a day. It was a hot and muggy August 16, 1977 and for a few hours we had been walking, sightseeing, touring and window shopping.

We were slowly walking along St. Antoine Steet heading towards the Champs de Mars Metro station, when a very old structure of a building housing a bookstore caught my eye. It was *Russell Books*.

Russell Books founded by Reginald Russell was a used second-hand bookstore and a Montreal institution for almost half a century.

The St. Antoine Street location was home to thousands of reasonably priced books, rare volumes and first editions. *Russell Books* closed in 1999.

I immediately grabbed Marie's hand and 'hauled' her into *Russell Books*. The book store was lined wall to wall with books; I was in 'book heaven'.

Because of Marie and her aching feet we only spent about a half hour to an hour browsing the many tables and many bookshelves of books.

Although our time spent at Russell Books was short, a hard cover edition of Don Bell's humorous *Saturday Night at the Bagel Factory and other Montreal stories* (1972) caught my eye. I gladly purchased the book.

Don Bell was a Montreal writer who stories appeared in *Weekend Magazine* and the *Montreal Star*.

Don Bell wrote the books *Saturday Night at the Bagel Factory and other Montreal stories* (1972) and *The Man Who Killed Houdini* (2004).

Don Bell passed away in 2003.

We left *Russell Books* and were walking along St. Antoine Street towards a Metro station when we heard an Elvis Presley song blasting from an approaching automobile. As the automobile sped by us and the Elvis Presley song faded in the distance, Marie and I continued to sing the words of the song. At one point I also began to play 'air guitar', pretending to be the 'King' himself in what must have been the worst Elvis Presley imitation of all time.

******

I arrived home at around 8:30 pm and walked towards the living room to greet my mother, and to let her know I was home. She was sitting on the sofa watching television, with tissues in hand and tears in her eyes.

I asked her what was wrong and she then informed me that Elvis Presley had passed away.

Elvis Aaron Presley (1935-1977), was an American singer and actor, referred to as 'the King of Rock and Roll'.

Elvis Presley was recognized worldwide for his many bestselling albums and countless singles such as 'Heartbreak Hotel' (1956), 'Love Me Tender' (1956), 'Hound Dog' (1956), 'Suspicious Minds' (1969), 'Always on My Mind' (1972), and 'Promised Land' (1974).

Elvis Presley also starred in the extremely successful films *Jailhouse Rock* (1957), *Viva Las Vegas* (1964), *Speedway* (1968). In 1968, following a break from live performances he returned in the comeback television special *Elvis*. Elvis also appeared in the first (via satellite) globally broadcast concert *Aloha from Hawaii* (1973).

Elvis Presley passed away August 16, 1977.

*****

Ronnie McDowell an American country music artist wrote and released the Elvis Presley tribute song 'The King is Gone' (1977).

Kurt Russell portrayed Elvis in the television biographical film *Elvis* (1979) directed by John Carpenter.

Michael St. Gerard starred as Elvis in the short lived ABC television series *Elvis* (1990), and Jonathan Rhys Meyers won an Emmy Award for his portray of Elvis in the CBS biographical *Elvis the mini-series* (2005).

While the world paid tribute and mourned the passing of Elvis Presley, Quebec was no exception. The province of Quebec has always held a special place in its heart for Elvis Presley.

The population of Quebec was in shock, people were openly crying and sharing stories about Elvis. Radio stations were playing his music and the television stations were keeping the public regularly informed with news bulletins and updates.

Quebec singer Johnny Farago wrote the French lyrics and recorded the personal and very touching 'La King N'est Plus' (1977), a French version of Ronnie McDowell's Elvis Presley tribute song 'The King Is Gone' (1977).

Johnny Farago (1944-1997) was a Quebec singer and a huge fan of Elvis Presley.

Discovered while still in his teens Johnny Farago joined the group Les Mercedes and in 1966 embarked on a solo career. He released 'Je T'Aime, Je Te Vieux' (1966) a French version of the Elvis Presley song 'I Want You, I Need You, I Love You.

Although he would sing in his natural voice and release many successful records, it was when he would cover or interpret an Elvis Presley song that he would imitate (in French) Elvis Presley's voice. That was the difference that set Johnny Farago apart from other Elvis Presley imitators/impersonators.

Johnny Farago released another Elvis Presley tribute song in both French 'Je Me Souviens D'Elvis Presley' (1978) and English 'I Remember Elvis Presley' (1978).

Sadly Johnny Farago passed away on July 31, 1997.

The world has seen its fair share of Elvis Presley imitators, impersonators, wantabe's and look alikes, some good, some not so good, some great, some not so great. David Scott was definitely the exception.

David Scott (1962-1993) was raised in Montreal and was a popular Elvis Presley impersonator appearing in Elvis Presley Tribute shows throughout Canada and the U.S.

Born out of wedlock, David Scott grew up believing a rumour that his mother had an affair with Elvis Presley a year before his birth and that he was the King's illegitimate son

David Scott appeared as an eighteen year old Elvis Presley in the documentary film 'This Is Elvis' (1981).

In 1989, he was performing and promoting a song he wrote 'I'm A Man' on television and concerts.

Early on in his career David Scott developed a drug habit and fell heavily into debt.

Sadly in 1993, according to news reports David Scott committed suicide in his Montreal home. David Scott was thirty years old.

chapter fourteen

I awoke to the sound of my alarm clock. I touched the off switch and turned the radio on. 98 CKGM morning man Ralph Lockwood was up to his usual tricks and hijinks. I could not help but think to myself how much of a joy it is to wake every morning to such a crazy and funny radio personality that is Ralph Lockwood.

I heard a knock, as my bedroom door was opening slightly ajar, it was my mother. "Good morning, just making sure you are awake. You start back at school today." She said a little too cheerfully. "I know Ma... I'm awake!" I responded not as cheerfully.

Lying on my back and staring at the ceiling, I was wondering to myself what this new school year would hold in store for me. Ralph Lockwood announced the next record as a Burton Cummings song, 'Never Had a Lady Before' (1977). I love the piano intro.

Canadian Burton Cummings was born (1947) in Winnipeg, Manitoba. He was singer/songwriter for the Guess Who a Canadian rock band.

In 1975, he launched a solo career and the Guess Who disbanded. He released his self-titled debut album and scored the international hit 'Stand Tall' (1976) and soon followed with 'I'm

Scared' (1976), 'Never Had a Lady Before' (1977), 'My Own Way To Rock' (1977).

The hits continued with 'Break It To Them Gently' (1978), 'Fine State Of Affairs' (1980), 'One And Only' (1980), 'You Saved My Soul' (1981), 'One Day Soon' (1990).

In 1982, Burton Cummings starred in the Canadian film *Melanie* co-starring Paul Sorvino, Don Johnson and Glynnis O'Connor. The *Melanie* soundtrack was supplied by Burton Cummings and featured the great 'Something Old, Something New' (1982).

In 2009, Burton Cummings was named an Officer of Canada and in 2011 he received a star on Canada's Walk of Fame.

I was still lying in bed as the song finished and a newscast anchored by veteran radio announcer Bill Roberts began. Bill Roberts began his news broadcast by announcing the uproar and anger Bill 101 was causing among the English speaking population of Quebec.

The Charter of the French Language (Bill 101) introduced by the Parti Quebecois, had officially become law on August 26, 1977.

Although French was already (Bill 22) the official language of the province of Quebec, Bill 101 made French the official language of government, courts and the workplace. Bill 101 also required that all signs be in French and all children attend French school (with the exception of those children who parents attended English school).

Bill 101 also established the Office Québécois de la Langue Française (aka the 'language police').

I thought of Marie and her family and wondered how or if Bill 101 would affect the stability of the plant where her father worked and the stability of the economy of Quebec.

I was also reflecting on these past few summer months that seemed to pass by so quickly and then decided to focus my attention to the coming school year.

I really should start thinking about my future and what I want to do when I finish school!" I thought to myself. I decided I would also make an appointment with the school guidance counsellor.

I rolled myself out of bed, took a quick shower, shaved, splashed some *Ice Blue Aqua Velva*, dressed, wished my mother a good day and set out to greet the first day of a new school year.

*****

First day back at school, sitting at a table in the cafeteria, and having a conversation with school friends, about what we had done during the summer months.

I explained that I did not really do much except pass the summer months working. I did not mention to my school mates that Marie and I had frequented each other.

I did however mention that I had gone to the Quebec Fête Nationale (English: Quebec National Holiday) festivities.

Quebec's la Fête Nationale (a paid statutory public holiday) is also (was previously) known as St. Jean Baptiste Day celebrated annually on June 24.
St. Jean Baptiste Day is a Christian feast day celebrating the birth of St. Jean Baptiste, a prophet who foretold the coming of the Messiah in the birth of Jesus, whom he later baptized.

The religious symbolism associated with the St. Jean Baptiste celebrations was eventually replaced with the political ideals of Quebec separation. In 1977, June 24 was declared Quebec's National Holiday.

The following week July 1, I attended a few Canada Day (French: Fête du Canada) celebrations.

Canada day, also known as Canada's birthday or the anniversary of Confederation is (a paid federal statutory holiday) celebrated annually on July 1.

Canada day celebrates the enactment of the Constitution Act, 1867 which united three colonies into a single country called Canada. The Constitution Act 1867 created Canada.

Other than that, the conversations were more or less the usual stories, with the exception of one. A friend mentioned that he had taken lessons and had begun to play the guitar. I mentioned that I had bought a used guitar at a garage sale and was 'strumming along' even composing a few original songs.

He mentioned that perhaps we should get together for a 'jamming' session. I chuckled to myself (never expecting to be a part of a 'jamming' session), I agreed.

*****

We met a few days later downstairs in his basement. He had invited another friend who had also begun playing guitar.

They both had electric guitars, and they both knew how to play, exchanging rhythms and riffs and guitar licks. I was way out of my league. I was surrounded by two excellent guitarists, and I had (strapped over my shoulders) my beaten up, out of tune, with one string missing, acoustic guitar.

To say that I was self-conscience and felt like an idiot would be an understatement. But at that very moment in time I felt something special in the air, and I knew that we would be making music and memories that would last us our entire lives.

We would practice every so often and eventually another friend who knew how to play drums joined us. He was an incredible drummer.

We would practice or 'jam' (actually the other musicians would 'jam'. I did not 'jam'. I was more of 'marmalade' or 'peanut butter' type guitar player) for the fun of it. It was a very enjoyable experience.

We would keep in touch after graduating senior high, and continued to practice together.

*****

A month into the new school year I met with the school guidance counsellor to determine what I would like to do or should do about my future.

The guidance counsellor was very patient and understanding as she explained to me the enrolment requirement for CEGEP (college) and/or the possibility of attending a trade school. To be honest, neither choice interested me. I really did not have a clue as to what I wanted to do or become. I was at a cross roads.

The guidance counsellor advised me to seriously think about my future and invited me back if I needed more consultations. She also stressed "that the next two years are going to fly by so fast."

How could two years fly by so fast I wondered?

fast forward three years:

Well...what can I say? The guidance counsellor was right and wrong! These past two years flew by without me realizing that it was three years. The past three years are almost a blur to me.

So what did happen in the last three years? Quite a bit!

Recollections, events, brief histories & trivia

👍☺ October 1977 Quebec's Gilles Villeneuve made his Formula One Canadian debut for Ferrari at the Canadian Grand Prix held at Mosport Park in Bowmanville, Ontario.

The Canadian Grand Prix (French: Grand Prix du Canada) is an auto race held annually in Canada.

In 1967 the race became part of the Formula One World Championship and was held mostly at Mosport Park in Bowanville, Ontario before safety concerns led the Canadian Grand Prix to move the race to its current home on Île Notre-Dame in Montreal (a circuit that would eventually be named after Gilles Villeneuve).

👍☺ In November 1977, with an attendance of over 68,000 at the Olympic Stadium, the Montreal Alouettes won their fourth Grey Cup by defeating the Edmonton Eskimos 41-6.

🗣️😟 The French language tabloid Montréal-Matin (1930-1978) folded.

👍☺️ During the 1977/78 hockey season The Montreal Canadiens once again beat the Boston Bruins in a best-of-seven series final (4 games to 2), winning their 21st Stanley Cup.

This would be the fourth Stanley Cup win for Montreal's head coach Scotty Bowman and the third in four consecutive Stanley Cup wins.

*****

Marie and I attended our senior prom together. The prom was held at the Queen Elizabeth Hotel in downtown Montreal. Marie looked stunningly beautiful, wearing a turquoise evening gown with the corsage I had given her. Marie was the prettiest young woman at our prom.

I did not rent a tuxedo from *Classy* like the other male graduates. I opted to wear a black suit, red shirt and black tie that I purchased at *A. Gold & Sons* (a men's clothing store chain) on rue Ste. Catherine.

I remember the salesman who served me would leave a lasting impression on me. The salesman took the time to show me an array of different attires in many colors, with different fabrics, various cuts and styles. He also showed me different varieties of men's casual wear.

"Clothes will always make the man." he said to me. He also advised me to "Dress the way you want to be perceived." Those few simple words of wisdom have remained with me my whole life.

Marie said I looked very handsome, the 'handsomest' of all the grads. Of course Marie was right.

We both had fun at our prom as we ate a nice meal, we mingled and joked with our fellow grads, we shared our hopes and aspirations for the future and more importantly we danced, but most of all we enjoyed each other's company.

My friend Joe also attended the prom with one of the many girlfriends he had been dating. Joe had become quite the "ladies man" and sometimes I found it a little difficult to keep track with the 'date-de-jour'.

At a pre-determined hour of the evening Marie and I decided to leave our prom and sneak off by ourselves. We walked to Old Montreal and decided on a guided horse-drawn carriage ride (French: *calèche*) through the old city.

The half-hour calèche ride was nice, Marie was feeling a little tired and laid her head on my shoulder. The late night air was cool, we kissed and we held each other tighter for warmth.

The calèche ride tour of Old Montreal was turning out to be very romantic and about come to an end when I jokingly whispered to Marie that she should have waited until the calèche ride was finished. Marie looked up to me and asked "What do you mean?"

I leaned into her and whispered "Your gassy." in her ear.

Anxious, red-faced, gasping for air and now gripping her nose between two fingers Marie said "You're the one who's gassy!"

At the exact same moment we both realized where the foul smelling stench was originating from, we both held our breath for dear life as the beautiful horse (I thought it was the horse that was 'gassy') and the somewhat scruffy looking carriage driver (while Marie thought it was the carriage driver who was 'gassy') continued to guide us through the cobbled streets of Old Montreal.

A good time was had by all.

*****

♪👍♫ Lisa Dal Bello's 'Still in Love with You' (1978) is a hit across Canada.

👍☺ With a 76-86 win/loss season and a fourth place finish in the National League Eastern Division, Montreal Expos starting pitcher Ross Grimsley won 20 games in 1978.

♪👍♫ One of my all-time favourite songs 'Is the Night Too Cold for Dancin'' (1978) by Randy Bachman (formerly of the Guess Who & Bachman-Turner Overdrive) is topping the music charts across Canada.

♪👍♫ Burton Cummings (also a former member of the Guess Who) is also topping the Canadian music charts with 'Break It To Them Gently' (1978).

👍☺ I graduated from senior high school in 1978. I applied and was accepted to Dawson College.

👍☺ Marie was also accepted to Dawson College, while my friend Joe decided to enrol in a trade school.

👍☺ *The Raes Variety Hour* (1978) was a musical/comedy summer replacement series from Vancouver, British Columbia that aired on the CBC Television Network.

The following season on CBC the variety show aired with a shortened title *The Raes* (1979-1980) in a half-hour format.

The Raes were Cherrill Yates from Ontario and Robbie Rae who grew up in Wales. The Raes met in England and upon moving to Canada were married. The single 'Que Sera Sera' (1977) a disco styled remake from their debut album was a hit across Canada.

The Raes hosted their own musical/comedy variety series on the CBC Television Network.

The Raes released their second album *Dancing Up a Storm* (1979) and the singles 'A Little Lovin' (Keeps the Doctor Away)'(1978) and '(I Only Wanna) Get Up and Dance'(1979).

Following the release of their third album *Two Heats*, Cherrill and Robbie Rae would split as a musical duo and eventually divorce.

🎵👍🎵 'Sweet Misery' (1978) by the Montreal based Teaze, is receiving radio airplay across Canada. Sweet Misery was produced by George Lagios and recorded at Aquarius records in Montreal.

👍☺ Montreal hosts its first Formula One Canadian Grand Prix in 1978. Due to safety concerns at the Mosport Park circuit in

Bowanville, Ontario, a new racetrack was constructed in Montreal and named Île Notre-Dame Circuit.

👍☺ Quebec's Gilles Villeneuve won his first Formula One Canadian Grand Prix in 1978. Gilles Villeneuve remains the only Canadian to win his home race.

Gilles Villeneuve (1950-1982) won six races for Ferrari in the six years he spent in Grand Prix. In 1982 he died during an accident of the final qualifying session for the Belgian Grand Prix at Zolder.

The racetrack on Île Notre-Dame was renamed in his honour as Circuit Gilles Villeneuve at the Canadian Grand Prix in 1982.

👍☺ November 1978, Jean Drapeau was re-elected as Mayor of Montreal.

👎☹ November 1978, the Edmonton Eskimos beat the Montreal Alouettes 20-13 to win the Grey Cup before 54,000 fans at Exhibition Stadium in Toronto.

*****

I graduated from senior high school in 1978. My grades were better than I thought they would be. I registered and was accepted to Dawson College. I also quit or if you prefer I 'dropped-out 'after two semesters.

Long story short: I didn't like the traveling from one campus to the other. Practically on a daily basis I would travel by bus and metro from the Viger Campus in Old Montreal to the Selby Campus in

Westmount, then the La Fontaine Campus on Sherbrooke Street East and finally to the Victoria Campus on McGill Street.

More often than not I would miss a bus and have to wait several minutes for another bus to arrive, or miss a metro train or the metro system would shut down and I would be late for class. Also carrying my school books back and forth from campus to campus wasn't much fun, so after two semesters, poor grades and a whole bunch of frustration, I deleted myself from the Social Science program at Dawson College.

Dawson College was the first English-language CEGEP (French: Collège d'enseignement général et professionnel) and opened in 1969. Eventually opening many campuses in and around downtown Montreal's surrounding area.

In order to unify its many campuses Dawson College acquired the Mother House of the Sisters of the Congrégation de Notre-Dame in 1981.

After a few years of extensive renovations of the century-old building, the campus opened in 1988.

Marie was studying hard and posting good grades at Dawson. She was fortunate as most of her classes or courses were mostly at one campus.

Lately Marie has been preoccupied. I guess because of CEGEP and her new surroundings, Marie always seemed to be busy, between attending CEGEP and homework Marie did not have too much time for me.

I did try my best to talk with and have a conversation with Marie concerning 'us' and our relationship. Again Marie seemed preoccupied. I did not pressure Marie instead I let Marie have her space.

Joe was also doing fine as he was attending a trade school.

After leaving Dawson College, I enrolled in a Driver Education Course at a neighbourhood driving school, passed my driver's test and received my driver's licence.

*****

👍☺ During the 1978/79 hockey season the Montreal Canadiens defeated the New York Rangers in a best-of-seven series final (5 games to 1), winning their 22nd Stanley Cup.

This would be the fifth Stanley Cup win for Montreal's head coach Scotty Bowman and the fourth in four consecutive Stanley Cup wins.

🎵👍🎵 A fifteen year old France Joli from Dorion, Quebec topped the international music charts with the disco hit 'Come To Me' (1979) written and produced by Montreal's Tony Green who also lent his vocal talents to the song.

🎵👍🎵 A fourteen year old Freddie James is also topping the international music charts with the Tony Green written and produced disco dance hit '(Everybody) Get Up and Boogie' (1979).

Freddie James was born (1965) in Chicago, Illinois and comes from a musical background. Freddie's mother, singer/songwriter

Geraldine Hunt relocated to Montreal, Quebec with her three kids in 1975.

Geraldine Hunt soon made a name for herself in Montreal when she released the French single 'J'ai Mal' (1976) and the *Sweet Honesty* (1978) album produced by Tony Green who would also produce her son Freddie James.

In 1980 Geraldine Hunt's second album *No Way* included the songs 'Glad, I'm In Love' (a personal favourite) and the internationally successful 'Can't Fake The Feeling'.

Geraldine's daughter Rosalind was one half of the music duo Cheri. Cheri released the international hit 'Murphy's Law' and followed up with the hit 'Star Struck' (1982) written by Geraldine Hunt, Freddie James and Peter Dowse.

Freddie James released the superb Tony Green produced *Come into the Jungle* (1993) on cd (compact disc). The single 'I Can't Get Enough (Of Your Love) was a favourite in the local club scene.

Geraldine Hunt, Freddie James and Rosalind Hunt have remained active in the Montreal music scene performing in nightclubs regularly.

Geraldine Hunt's third child, Jeanne Croteau is a writer, a professor and mother of four.

Author's note:

Come into the Jungle has always been a personal favourite of mine; it's an album that I still listen to today.

Perhaps due in part to the lack of promotion and poor distribution of the album by its record label, *Come into the Jungle* failed to sell, and went virtually unnoticed upon its release.

Come into the Jungle is a masterpiece of an album featuring a fine collection of quality songs showcasing the soulful vocal talents of Freddie James.

Come into the Jungle should have been a huge international success; it deserved a much better fate than what it received.

*****

☺ May 22, 1979, after 11 years in power Pierre Elliot Trudeau's Liberal Party of Canada were defeated by the Joe Clark led Progressive Conservative Party.

☺ June 4, 1979, with a minority government Progressive Conservative leader Joe Clark was sworn in as Canada's 16th Prime Minister.

☺ Scotty Bowman stepped down as coach of the Montreal Canadians to become coach and General Manager of the Buffalo Sabres.

☺ 1979, the World Hockey Association merged with the National Hockey League.

Four WHA teams the Edmonton Oilers, the Quebec Nordiques, the Winnipeg Jets and the New England Whalers renamed the Hartford Whalers joined the NHL.

☺ September 1979 the broadsheet Montreal Star ceased publication.

☺ 1979 the Montreal Expos challenged for the National League Eastern Division Title all the way until the final weekend of the season, before, finishing with a franchise best 95-65 record, and finishing one game behind the eventual World Champions Pittsburgh Pirates.

🐟☹ November 25, 1979, with an attendance of over 65,000, the Edmonton Eskimos beat the Montreal Alouettes 17-9 to win the Grey Cup at the Olympic Stadium in Montreal.

📖❓☺ December 13, 1979, an election is called as Prime Minister Joe Clark's Progressive Conservative government is defeated on a non-confidence motion.

📖🐾☺ January 27, 1980 (soon to become known as the Canadian Caper) six American diplomats posing as Canadians secretly escape Tehran during the Iran Hostage Crisis.

> On November 4, 1979, a mob of Iranians, radical university students and supporters of the Ayatollah Khomeini aggressively stormed (and later occupied) the American Embassy in Tehran, Iran holding 52 Americans hostage for 444 days (November 4, 1979 to January 20, 1981).
>
> Within the confusion of the hostage taking, six Americans casually escaped from the American Embassy and after hiding out for four days asked the Canadian Embassy for sanctuary.
>
> Ken Taylor the Canadian Ambassador to Iran informed the Canadian government of the situation and a plan of secrecy including forged Canadian passports was soon set in motion through cooperation between the Canadian and U.S. governments.

The process of closing down the Canadian Embassy had slowly begun and staff members gradually began to depart. 79 days later on January 27, 1980, the six American 'houseguests' (posing as Canadians) and the remaining Canadian Embassy staff left Tehran.

The daring rescue brought an outpouring of gratitude from the United States.

Jean Pelletier then Washington correspondent for the Quebec newspaper La Presse (through 'guesswork' had known about the American 'houseguests') broke the story on January 29, 1980.

Jean Pelletier wrote the superb book *The Canadian Caper* (1981) with Claude Adams.

Canadian actor Gordon Pinsent portrayed Ken Taylor in the dramatized CTV television film *Escape from Iran: The Canadian Caper* (1981).

February 18, 1980 in a Canadian Federal Election, Pierre Elliot Trudeau led his Liberal party to victory over the Progressive Conservatives.

April 12, 1980 Terry Fox embarks on his Marathon of Hope (a cross-country run to raise money for Cancer Research) in St. John's Newfoundland.

In April 1980 the Parti Québécois government announced the date for the upcoming Quebec referendum as May 20, 1980.

chapter fifteen

Due to the upcoming Quebec Referendum many businesses and companies were closing, moving and relocating.

The import/export company that my sister Ellen was employed at extended to her, a raise and continued employment if she was willing to relocate once its Montreal office closed and the company moved to Toronto.

After much thought and with my mother's support Ellen accepted the job offer and made up her mind to relocate. Ellen's boyfriend was a little reluctant but soon changed his mind to join Ellen in her move Toronto.

My brother George was still employed and was now in a relationship.

My mother was sad but understood and supported the reasons behind Ellen's moving to Toronto, Ontario.

The family of my friend Joe were also set to move out to Alberta, Calgary. Joe felt he was not ready to move since he still had a few months left to complete his trade course to become an electrician.

His father offered to set Joe up in an apartment downtown until he graduated from his electrician course.

I was still working at the Texan and still trying to figure out what I should do with my life. With the political instability in Quebec I was also torn as to what I should be doing. So I continued to work hard and coast along.

Lately Marie has been preoccupied, and moody. I guess because of CEGEP and her surroundings, Marie always seemed to be busy, between attending CEGEP and homework Marie did not have too much time for me.

I did try my best to talk with and have a conversation with Marie concerning 'us' and our relationship. Again Marie seemed preoccupied. I did not pressure Marie instead I let Marie have her space.

We did however spend a nice evening celebrating our eighteenth birthday's (our birthdays were ten days apart) at the *Kon Tiki* in the Sheraton-Mt. Royal Hotel. The *Kon Tiki's* entrance was on Peel Street in downtown Montreal.

The Kon Tiki opened in 1958 and was a Montreal landmark. The Kon Tiki featured Exotic South Seas Dining and equally exotic drinks.

The décor was definitely exotic in that the Kon Tiki was windowless. Enhancing the dark atmosphere were dark walls, palms, lagoons and multi-colour lightning. The Kon Tiki was a Montreal favourite meeting place for many years.

The Kon Tiki closed in 1983.

That night at the *Kon Tiki* Marie did confide in me the reason why she was distant or preoccupied. Regardless of the outcome of the approaching 1980 Quebec Referendum, Marie's family had decided to leave Montreal for Toronto. Marie and her family would be moving in July.

I must admit that I was not really surprised by the news.

I explained to Marie that I understood and reassured her that her place was with her family. I also confided to Marie that my sister Ellen and that Joe's family as well were also leaving the province. Marie was saddened by the news.

I ordered another Mai Tai for me and a Barbados Swizzle for Marie.

chapter sixteen

I went to work one Thursday night at the Texan, Theodore the day time dishwasher was waiting for me. Theodore (an elderly gentleman) asked me to replace him on his Saturday shift explaining that a family emergency had come up. I reassured him that it was not a problem. Theodore was thankful and extended an open invitation to pass by the *Guy Cinema* on Guy Street.

Theodore explained that he was the night manager at the *Guy Cinema* and anytime I wanted to view a movie, he would let me in free of charge. I thanked him.

A week or so later, the day before the 1980 Quebec Referendum, I was with my friend Joe downtown, (we were 'apartment hunting' for Joe whose family were preparing to relocate to Alberta) and we walked past the *Guy Cinema*, I stopped and entered the cinema to say 'Hello' to my co-worker Theodore.

He was happy to see me and asked if I wanted to watch the movie that was playing, I looked over to my friend Joe and he nodded affirmatively.

Theodore smiled and with a flashlight in hand led us to a seat in the movie theatre.

The theatre was dark and as we were settling into our seats we both could hear moaning and groaning. We glanced behind us but could not see the couple making the sounds. Finally settled in our seats we both looked towards the viewing screen. Surprise, surprise… We were both pleasantly shocked!

On screen were a naked couple, next to them another naked couple besides another naked couple, on a huge bed groaning and moaning. There were men and women having sex on screen. Not 'performing sex' but actually having sex on screen, before my very eyes. My friend Joe and I soon realized that we were in an adult movie theatre, watching an adult film.

The star of the adult film was obviously the beautiful, sexy platinum blonde who was interacting and intermingling with the three couples.

I was taught in high school about sexual relationships or 'the birds and the bees' but the adult film I was viewing was a whole lot more descriptive, visual and self-explanatory. As a gesture of respect (ahem) towards Theodore, my friend Joe and I stayed until the end of the movie.

Approaching the exit, Theodore greeted us with a huge grin on his face. We thanked him for the movie and left the *Guy Cinema* (promising ourselves to return).

Outside while looking over the framed movie posters, I lit myself a cigarette. The film we had just viewed was *Ultra Flesh*, and the incredibly sexy platinum-blonde goddess who starred in the movie was simply named Seka.

During the 1970's and early 1980's, Seka was the reigning queen and brought a certain respectability to the Adult Film Industry.

Seka, by far the most popular porn star of all time starred in over fifty adult films and also directed the adult films *Inside Seka* and *Careful He May Be Watching*.

I returned on a few more occasions (strictly for educational purposes) to the *Guy Cinema*.

Little did I know that in a very short period of time, the 'educational film' I had witnessed on screen and what I had learned from the film, would soon be put to use.

*****

newsflash

Extra! Extra! Read all about it...

The province-wide referendum took place on Tuesday, May 20, 1980 and was held to decide on the place of the province of Quebec within Canada and whether the province of Quebec should pursue a path toward sovereignty.

The province-wide referendum and the proposal to pursue secession were defeated by a vote of 59.56 percent to 40.44 percent margin.

chapter seventeen

With the province wide Quebec referendum over and done with (or was it? There would be a second referendum in 1995) city life in Montreal slowly returned to 'normal'.

My sister Ellen with her boyfriend had already moved (May 1980) to Toronto.

My mother continued with her days as she did before but my brother George and I could feel the change in my mom. She seemed sad and lonely and she did not seem to have much to say. More and more she kept to herself.

Joe's family moved to Alberta (June 1980) and Joe was to join then around the first week of August once he was finished his schooling. Joe's father was able to strike a deal (without signing a one year lease) for a furnished apartment on rue St. Marc in downtown Montreal; he paid six months (June –November) in advance even though Joe would be leaving in August

Joe and I attended (via closed circuit) the sporting event of the year, 'The Brawl in Montreal'.

Sugar Ray Leonard would return to Montreal on June 20, 1980 to defend his WBC Welterweight Championship title against challenger Roberto Duran.

Although Sugar Ray toke the fight to Roberto Duran, Duran was much too powerful for Sugar Ray.

Sugar Ray Leonard lost the fight in a unanimous decision, in front of a crowd of over 44,000 at Montreal's Olympic Stadium.

In the undercard for the Leonard/Duran fight, 'Big' John Tate lost by knock-out to up and coming Trevor Brebick.

The countdown for Marie's family relocating to Toronto had begun. The days were passing us by very quickly. July was approaching at top speed. Then something surprising happened.

It was near the end of June; Marie phoned to inform me that her parents would be spending the weekend in Toronto. They needed to clear-up some last minute details, before the 'move'.

She also wanted to talk to me.

*****

We eventually met and Marie explained that she was grateful for my friendship and although she was sad and still a little angry about leaving Montreal, she had come to terms with the situation.

She continued that she had been thinking about something the last few weeks and decided that she would like for me to be her first.

Even though Marie and I had been close these last couple of years, sexually we were both inexperienced.

155

Sure we were affectionate towards one another and yes we did have our romantic and passionate moments and on occasion discussed being intimate but we also agreed that when the 'time' was right we would both know it.

'You're first? You're first what?" I questioned. Of course I knew what Marie was suggesting, I was pretending to be 'clueless'.

"David, think about it." she said softly, reaching for my hand.

"Marie, I don't understand. You're first what?" I was totally confused and becoming frustrated.

"David!" she reached up her right hand to my face and gave my right cheek two small taps. "David, listen to me closely. Pay close attention to what I am saying." she said firmly but softly.

"Marie, I am." I stated.

"David, I do not want to remain a virgin." she said casually. "I want you to be my first!"

Searching Marie's eyes I knew what she was saying. My ears did not believe it. Finally I said to Marie "Are you sure?" she nodded her head yes. "Do you understand what you are asking of me?" Again she nodded yes.

"So…when?" I asked. Marie responded "This week while my parents are in Toronto."

I remained as cool as I possibly could be. Inside, I was a tap dancer clicking my heels.

*****

Thankfully the week-end took it's time to arrive. I had so much to do; go to the barber for a haircut, buy a bouquet of flowers and a box of Laura Secord chocolates.

Laura Secord Chocolates was founded in 1913 by Frank P. O'Connor and named in honour of Laura Secord, a Canadian heroine of the War of 1812 in the region of Queenston (Niagara Peninsula).

Laura Secord, after overhearing a discussion of a planned American surprise attack on a British outpost, and fearing the fall of the Niagara Peninsula to the Americans, set out (on an 18 hour, 32-kilometre trek) to alert authorities of the pending attack. Laura Secord's trek would save both British and Canadian forces. Two days later the Americans were intercepted and surrendered at the Battle of Beaver Dams.

Laura Secord is Canada's largest chocolatier with over 120 stores. Laura Secord sells an affordable variety of premium quality chocolates.

I borrowed a few of my mother's Dean Martin records (to set a romantic mood) and I also needed to purchase a few prophylactics or condoms.

I chuckled to myself, as I remembered a year or so earlier when I thought perhaps Marie and I were going to become intimate. I had gone to a local pharmacy establishment, walked up and down the aisles searching for prophylactics. I couldn't find a box of condoms on any of the shelves and finally decided to ask for help. There was a pharmacy employee in the next aisle kneeling down replacing inventory on a shelf.

I interrupted him and informed him that I wanted to purchase a box of condoms. The employee explained that the prophylactics were not stocked on the aisle shelves; I would have to go ask for a box at the cash counter at the front of the store. The employee also added that he thought maybe I was a little young to be purchasing prophylactics.

Really? Am I too young? Maybe I am! I thought to myself. What to do? What to do? Should I ask my brother George to buy the condoms for me? No, he would blab to my mother. What to do? What to do? Then the light turned on in my head. I knew what to do!

I waited outside the pharmacy establishment, and solicited strangers to purchase the condoms for me. Many of the strangers (all male) I asked were not interested in purchasing condoms for me. One older gentleman gave me a 'look' and a lecture, stating I was too young to be engaging in a sexual relationship. Jokingly, the elder gentleman proclaimed that he himself was too young to be in a sexual relationship. I thought he was a funny man; he made me chuckle to myself.

One person, male, in his late twenties seemed to be amused by my request. He asked me if I wanted a package of three condoms or a box of twelve. Lubricated or regular! Decisions, decisions… I thought to myself, as I slipped him the money and requested a box of twelve lubricated condoms.

Outside he handed me the bag containing the condom box and told me to "Knock yourself out."

It was a little embarrassing to have to ask a complete stranger to purchase condoms for me but the cause at that time was right just like it is now.

*****

I checked the expiration date on the box of condoms I had purchased a year or so earlier and thought it best to purchase another box.

I was downtown walking on rue Sainte Catherine and entered a pharmacy, went to the cash counter and asked for a box of twelve condoms. The big breasted dark haired cashier with the milky white skin asked if I wanted "lubricated?" I replied that I did.

She turned behind her and asked "Any particular brand?"

"No not really, any brand would do…"

The cashier reached for a box and as she returned to face me the box of condoms slipped from her hand and fell to the floor behind the counter. She excused herself and instinctively bent over to pick up the box. As she was leaning over, a button from the turquoise blouse she was wearing unfastened, exposing the most beautiful breast cleavage.

The cashier hadn't noticed that a button from her blouse was unfastened and I couldn't help but enjoy the 'jiggling' of cleavage as she preceded to place the box of condoms in a brown paper bag.

She entered the price of purchase into the cash register and then realised I was a little flushed and gawking at her (in a nonchalant way). The cashier was about to say something when she refastened the button of her blouse and handed me the paper bag.

Without making eye contact I could feel the cashier looking straight at me as I reached for the paper bag. The cashier asked if I was alright and I responded that I was. She informed me of the purchase price; I reached into my front pants pocket, pulled out my billfold and paid for the condoms.

The week-end was tomorrow. I just had one more thing to do…

*****

Later that evening I went to see Theodore at the *Guy Cinema*. He escorted me to a seat, I thanked him. I sat down and made myself comfortable. I needed to pay very close attention to the screen.

first time episode

The following day, an hour or so before I was to meet Marie, I took a quick shower and a shave. I was almost ready to leave (to meet Marie) but not before splashing my face with a little of my Aqua Velva Ice Blue aftershave.

It's soothing, cooling, refreshing sensation and manly scent encouraged my self-confidence. I was ready to greet the day.

As I was walking to Marie's, I could not help but think and replay in my mind the events leading to today. Slowly my walking pace increased and the Aqua Velva jiggle entered my mind, smiling, I sang to myself *"There's something about an Aqua Velva man"*.

I arrived at Marie's, it was late afternoon. She greeted me with a kiss and commented "You smell really nice, David" and led me into the living room. We sat on the sofa and talked a while. I questioned her if she still felt comfortable with what she had asked of me. She assured me she was.

I asked Marie if she would like to listen to some music, she responded "Sure, is the radio okay?" I handed her, Dean Martin's Greatest Hits on vinyl. She looked at the record album and exclaimed "Dean Martin? My parents listen to him sometimes. Is this what you really want to listen to?" I nodded yes.

She looked at me, and then back to the album cover, 'rolled her eyes' shrugged her shoulders and turned to the living room record player. I assured her that "I am just trying to create a mood to help us feel more comfortable." From over her shoulder I heard her say "Okay, if you say so..."

Dean Martin (1917-1995) was an American singer, comedian and actor. In 1946, Dean Martin and Jerry Lewis formed a partnership appearing in clubs, on radio, television and in film as the comedy duo Martin & Lewis. The comedy duo broke up in 1956 and both performers embarked on successful solo careers.

Dean Martin performed in Las Vegas as a solo performer and as a member of the 'Rat Pack' with Frank Sinatra, Sammy Davis Jr., Peter Lawford and Joey Bishop.

As an actor, Dean Martin appeared in over fifty motion pictures. He starred in the film *Ocean's Eleven* (1960) with his fellow 'Rat Packers' and also starred in a series of four spy spoofed film adaptions *The Silencers* (1966), *Murderer's Row* (1966), *The Ambushers* (1967) and *The Wrecking Crew (1968)* of Donald Hamilton's American secret agent Matt Helm. Dean Martin's last leading role was in the crime drama *Mr.Ricco* (1975).

On television, *The Dean Martin Show* (1964-1974) was a weekly comedy-variety show which would morph into *The Dean Martin Celebrity Roast* (1974-1984).

Musically Dean Martin recorded many studio albums and released many hit singles 'Volare' (1958), 'Everybody Loves Somebody' (1963), 'Sway' (1953), 'That's Amore' (1953) and 'Mambo Italiano' (1955).

Dean Martin is also known as 'The King of Cool'. Indeed he is. Dean Martin passed away in 1995.

Marie re-joined me on the sofa, and I gave her the bouquet of flowers and the Laura Secord box of chocolates. She thanked me and kissed me on the lips.

While 'Dino' sang in the background we embraced, kissed and then began kissing passionately. My hands slowly began to move their way over her body, touching and feeling her every curve.

We were both breathing heavily as we began to undress one another. Marie's body was absolutely fantastic. She had shapely curves in all the right places. I was so excited.

With the Dean Martin record playing in the background, the mood was set. I suggested to Marie that we take a shower together. She was a little hesitant, but soon agreed.

While Marie fiddled with the shower faucet, I was first in the shower, naked. Marie's facial expression was priceless as she shyly looked at my nude body. "Oh, my…" was all she said.

Warm to hot water sprayed down on me from the shower head, as Marie joined me. We embraced for what seemed to be an eternity.

I reached for a bar of soap and began to lather Marie's lovely firm body.

Marie followed my lead, lathering my neck, my shoulders, my arms and my chest, stopping momentarily at my stomach.

She looked in my eyes then turned away, she then turned back to me, with the bar of soap still in her grasp, and she then continued to lather the rest of my body.

We towelled each other dry. I asked Marie if she was alright, and she responded that she was.

"I am just a little frightened, this is my first time. I am not really sure what I should be doing." she stated.

"You are doing fine." I assured her. "Relax, don't worry, I've seen a few films." We then entered her bedroom, closing the bedroom door behind us.

Fast-forward:
2 minutes later.

I was breathing heavy, panting and lying on my back. My heart was racing; my body was dripping sweat onto Marie's bed sheets.

Marie with her head on my left shoulder was staring aimlessly.

"Are you okay?" I asked (huffing and puffing).

"I'm fine, really." she whispered.

"Any regrets?" I inquired (still huffing and puffing).

"Everything is fine…" she said calmly, and then continued "I just thought there would have been more to it…"

I turned my face sideways and kissed the top of Marie's head. I did not understand. Confused by her comments, I replayed her voice and what she said in my mind. "More to it…"

I was looking up towards the bedroom ceiling, and soon realized that I was also staring aimlessly. Dumbfounded… I questioned myself.

What did she mean by "More to it?"

chapter eighteen

July came and went, Marie and her family moved to Toronto. Marie promised that she would write me with news, she wanted us to continue to be friends as 'pen pals' at least. It has been a month and I have not received a letter from Marie.

Joe was mentally set to leave but until then he was making the most of his downtown apartment. Joe had turned into quite the 'ladies' man' and he seemed (or so he bragged) to be with a different woman almost every night.

As for me I need to keep busy so I enrolled in a two month introductory accounting course.

*****

One Sunday afternoon, I just finished a work shift at the *Texan* when Nick, (a co-worker) suggested that we go to the *Montreal Pool Room* for a couple of 'steamies'.

The *Montreal Pool Room* is probably best described as a greasy spoon (French: casse-croûte) which serves the best 'steamies' (steamed hot-dogs served in a steamed bun) in Montreal. The *Montreal Pool Room* is located in Montreal's (then) 'red-light district', Saint Laurent and Saint Catherine's Street.

The term Red Light recalls one of the old lanterns on the doors of brothels. Historically the neighbourhood had been home to cabarets, gambling, illicit taverns, prostitution and the selling of drugs.

In recent years the *Montreal Pool Room* was one of several businesses that resisted attempts to redevelop and gentrify the district and surrounding area. Since then the *Montreal Pool Room* has moved (from its original location) across the street.

The *Montreal Pool Room* has been opened to the public since 1912, serving steamed hot-dogs, burgers, 'patates frites' (French fries) and poutine to its many satisfied customers.

Nick and I walked a block to the *Alexis Nihon Plaza* (a shopping center complex across the street from or facing the *Montreal Forum*), and entered the Atwater Metro station. It was while we were waiting for the Metro train to arrive that Nick suggested a change in plans.

Our original destination was to go to the *Montreal Pool Room* on Saint Laurent, so were to get off at Saint Laurent metro station and walk south to the *Montreal Pool Room*. Nick suggested that we get off at Place des Arts metro station. Nick wanted to stop in at the *Trident* before the *Montreal Pool Hall*.

I had never heard of the *Trident* but tagged along. The *Trident* was located on rue Saint Catherine near rue Bleury. The *Trident*, I soon realised was a bar. Nick explained that he knew the doorkeeper. Doorkeeper! I thought to myself.

We entered the *Trident Bar* and were welcomed by the doorkeeper, who greeted Nick with a big smile and a firm handshake. After a few minutes of idle conversation, Nick introduced me to his friend Frank; we shook hands while Frank the doorkeeper escorted us to a table for two.

At first glance the *Trident Bar* was dark, poorly lite with a few flashing lights, and short on décor. Disco music was blasting loud around us. There were also a handful of patrons in attendance.

As I sat down the doorkeeper Frank leaned in and whispered in my ear that "It's customary to tip the doorman." I stood up and reached into my pocket for some change when Frank said "A dollar will do." I nodded affirmatively and reached in my right pocket for my billfold.

I explained to Frank that I only had a two dollar bill and he said it was okay, that he would give me change in return. I handed a two dollar bill to Frank as he gave me a pat on the back, wished me a good time and walked back towards the entrance of the bar.

Frank the doorkeeper did not return with the change from the two dollar bill I gave him.

I sat back down, looked at Nick who was smiling, and glanced around at the décor. I was just about to offer a cigarette to Nick when a red bikini wearing woman with big breasts and a shapely body approached our table and asked us what we would like to order. Nick leaned in her direction, I didn't hear what he said to her but she soon departed, only to reappear with two glasses of ice cubes filled with cola.

She placed the two glasses of ice cubes filled with cola on the table, looked at me then at Nick who handed her a five dollar bill and suggested she keep the change.

Nick offered me one of the drinks and we clicked the two glasses in a toast to good health. Nick drank a large mouthful of cola and replaced the now half-empty glass in front of him. I also took a sip of cola but soon released that the cola had a bit of a 'kick' to it.

The glass of cola did not taste bad or foul, just different then what I was used to. The drinks at the *Kon Tiki* were 'fancier' and more exotic than what I was now drinking at the Trident. Nick looked at me and smiled. I took a larger sip. Nick asked me if I liked the drink and I responded that it was alright. He explained that I was drinking a 'rum and coke', a drink that was his preference. I took a larger sip and continued to look around my surroundings.

The music in the bar was loud and seemed to surround us (the bar had a great speaker system), France Joli's 'Come To Me' was playing and I noticed that some tables had wooden boxes placed next to them. The wooden boxes must have measured two feet wide by three feet long and one foot high.

I asked Nick what the boxes were for and he responded to "Wait and you will see my friend." I shrugged my shoulders and finished my 'rum and coke'.

There was a huge circular stage in the middle of the Trident, with flashing lights and two metal poles, one at each end of the stage. A few patrons were seated on metal chairs (which encircled the stage) drinking, and smoking. Oh…and there was a shapely woman swaying, dancing and disrobing to the beat of the music.

I reached into my pocket and pulled out a pack of cigarettes and offered one to Nick, who readily accepted.

Another round of drinks soon followed, I was just becoming accustomed to my surroundings when a wooden box was placed directly in front of me. I looked over to Nick with a questioning look and he just shrugged his shoulders.

The intro to Claudja Barry's 'Dancin' Fever' (1977) had begun just as a petit dark skinned woman wearing a light orange bikini approached me and extended her hand for me to help or steady her as she mounted the wooden box.

She leaned forward and introduced herself as Yolanda and began to sway to the infectious rhythm.

Claudja Barry was born in Jamaica and raised in Canada. She released a few record albums and the huge disco dance hits 'Dancin' Fever' (1977) and 'Johnny Johnny Please Come Home' (1977). Her biggest hit was 'Boogie Woogie Dancin' Shoes' (1978).

As the song 'Dancin' Fever' played on, Yolanda rhythmically undressed, first removing seductively her bikini top, one cup at a time revealing her small but firm beasts in a teasing way. I was sitting in my chair, enjoying the seduction that was Yolanda.

I was beginning to feel a little uncomfortable. I realised that I was becoming sexually aroused. I reach for my drink and took a sip, hoping that my 'uncomfortability' would go unnoticed.

I replaced my drink on the table and noticed that Nick was wearing a huge smile. I returned my attention to Yolanda who was now slowly removing her bikini bottom; exposing the most beautiful 'backside' I had ever seen.

Yolanda's 'backside' was mesmerizing, moving back and forth and up and down. I was now under the spell of seduction that was the incredible naked woman Yolanda.

The palms of my hands were sweaty and I could feel beads of sweat forming on my forehead. My lips were dry and I tried my best to moisten them with my tongue, hoping that Yolanda would not see me moistening them.

The opened collar blue shirt I was wearing, for some reason felt like a turtleneck sweater. My throat was dry and my body felt tight, yet I could not take my eyes off of Yolanda's perfect 'backside'.

The loose fitting pair of denim blue jeans I was wearing, now felt tight and uncomfortable around the crouch area. Hoping for a little relief I tried shifting in my chair, but to no avail. Luckily (or was it?) the song ended and Yolanda dismounted the wooden box. She asked if I wanted another dance.

I did not hear or understand what Yolanda had asked me. I was still in a trance and now enjoying the full frontal view of Yolanda's completely naked body. Again she asked if I wanted another dance to which I did not respond. How could I respond? I was transfixed on her nakedness.

At first I thought I felt a light tap on my shoulder, and then I felt a hand gently shaking my shoulder. It was Yolanda and she was asking if I was okay. I forced my eyes away from her full frontal nakedness and focused my eyesight towards her pretty face; she was very, very pretty.

Yolanda was smiling at me and again asked if I was okay.

"Oh yes of course I am why wouldn't I be? I responded.

"Are you sure?" She replied as I again shifted in my chair, "Of course I am!" I said matter-of-factly.

"Okay then, the dance will be five dollars." She said as she slowly bent over to pick-up her light orange bikini from the wooden box.

Sometimes a man's eyes are an entity of their own as my eyes were once again transfixed on Yolanda's bent over beautiful backside. Talk about a 'full moon'!

She straightened herself and put on her bikini top, adjusting her firm boobs as she did so. She then reached for her bikini bottom and slowing stepped into it, one beautiful leg at a time.

'That will be five dollars." She stated while looking at me.

"Oh yes," mumbling "For the dance." I said as I attempted to stand and reach into my pocket for my billfold, then realizing that I would not be able to fully rise and/or stand because of an erection hidden in my denim jeans. Or was it hidden?

I heard Yolanda quietly exclaim "Oh my!" and with a kittenish smile she gestured me to remain seated.

"You should relax for a little while; I'll come back in a few minutes." Confused by what she said I questioned her. "Why would you come back when I can pay you now?'

Again I attempted to rise from my seat but again felt the tightness of my jeans hold me back. Yolanda leaned closer into me and pointing casually towards my crouch, Yolanda whispered "That's a big reason why!"

A little embarrassed and a little self-conscious I accepted Yolanda's advice and remained seated, I glanced across the table to Nick who was (thankfully) not there.

Yolanda suggested a drink might steady my sexual 'arousalness' and in agreement I ordered three drinks, one for each of us. Yolanda said she would be right back, turned and began walking towards the bar. Yes of course I watched her walk away.

Nick reappeared at the table and explained he had gone to the washroom. I told him that I ordered us a couple more drinks and asked where the wash room was located

The Trident washroom was small in size with two bathroom stalls and three urinals. I splashed some cold water on my face and returned to the table. Yolanda had returned with our drinks and was waiting my return.

As I was approaching the table, Yolanda was approaching me. "I see you are able to walk now!" She said playfully "You were in the washroom for a long time I was beginning to think you needed some help doing what it was you were doing." I chuckled as I continued to the table. Yolanda followed behind me. At the table I reached into my right jeans pocket and pulled out my billfold.

"I was just splashing water on my face, was I in the washroom that long?" I asked.

"Yes you were…I was about to go in and give you a helping hand…oh well, maybe next time." She said coyly. I sensed she was flirting with me.

I continued to flirt and pressed on "When, will next time be?" I think I caught her off guard with my question, she did not respond. I opened my billfold, pulled out a twenty dollar bill and offered it to her for the dance and drinks.

"Twenty should be enough for the dance and drinks." I said. She took the twenty dollar bill and replied "More than enough. Let me give you your change." I sat down and said "No, no you can keep the change."

She nodded her head affirmatively, thanked me for her drink, wished me a good time and slowly walked away.

Nick was all smiles as we 'clicked' our glasses in a silent toast. He asked "You paid for the dance?" I responded that I did. Nick said that he wanted to treat me to the dance which is why he had motioned to the dancer to place the wooden box at my seat. I thanked him. I took a huge mouthful of my drink, which I would soon finish. I said to Nick I was hungry and he agreed that he was also hungry.

Nick suggested instead of going to the Montreal Pool Room that we should walk up rue St. Laurent and grab ourselves a Smoked-meat sandwich at Schwartz's. I had never been there but agreed.

We finished our drinks and began walking towards the exit. I was feeling a little light-headed and my legs were weak, when Yolanda approached me and asked if we were leaving. I said that we were and she invited me to "Come and see me anytime." I glanced to Nick who was now talking with his friend Frank, the doorkeeper. I returned my glance to Yolanda and thanked her for her hospitality.

Moving in closer to me, Yolanda said "You are very welcome and I do hope you will come see me again." She turned and slowly walked away. I stood there admiring her beautiful, perfect 'backside' in the light orange bikini walking away. I just couldn't help myself.

I would visit Yolanda on many occasions.

****

Apparently standing in line outside *Schwartz's Hebrew Delicatessen* is a common occurrence, in part because *Schwartz's* is considered to serve the 'best' smoked-meat sandwiches, so people are willing to wait in line. Another reason for the long line-ups is the limited number of tables partly because the local is not very spacious.

Nick and I had just finished smoking a cigarette when we were signalled into *Schwartz's* as a few seats had become available.

The aroma of smoked-meat attacked us as soon as we entered *Schwartz's*. We were led to an already occupied table that had two available chairs; we sat down and glance around at the decorated walls.

The waiter arrived quickly to ask us our order; Nick and I both ordered a medium smoked-meat sandwich with mustard, fries and a black cherry soda.

The waiter had not been gone but a minute when he reappeared with our order, wished us a 'bonne appetite' and left to serve other customers. I was famished as I grabbed one half of my sandwich in my hands and bit into it. There is nothing better than a good Montreal smoked-meat sandwich.

Smoked-meat is a kosher-style deli meat product created by salting and curing or dry-curing beef brisket (a cut of meat from the breast or lower chest of beef) with spices.

The brisket absorbs the flavours for at least a week, then hot-smoked (exposes the brisket to smoke and heat in a controlled environment) and is then hung to develop a coating and then smoked. Montreal smoked-meat should always be sliced warm and by hand (against the grain) to maintain its form.

A Montreal smoked-meat sandwich is built on rye bread, stacked with hand-sliced smoked meat topped with yellow prepared mustard. Et voila the perfect sandwich!

Montreal has been home to many delicatessens or deli's over the years. Much debate has also gone on for years as to which deli served the best smoked meat sandwiches.

- *Schwartz's Montreal Hebrew Delicatessen* on rue St. Laurent, was established in 1928 by Reuben Schwartz. The deli has had a handful of different owners since its opening. Schwartz's is probably the most famous Montreal delicatessen.

- *Ben's Delicatessen and Restaurant* was situated on De Maisonneuve Boulevard near rue Metcalfe, was established in 1908 by Benjamin Kravitz. Ben's employees unionized in 1995 and in 2006 voted to strike, Ben's closed and did not reopen.

- *Chenoy's Delicatessen* originally opened on St. Laurent near Marieanne Street in 1936. There have been franchises throughout the years.

- *Main Deli Steak House* on rue St. Laurent opened in 1974, and has been a competitor/alternative to Schwartz's.

- *Dunn's Famous Restaurant* was founded by Myer Dunn in 1927. There have been franchises throughout the years.

I have frequented these delicatessens over the years and they all serve a very good smoked meat sandwich. My preference hands down, would be *Brisket Montréal Salon Krausmann* on cote de Beaver Hall. Their smoked meat sandwich is full of flavour and melts in your mouth.

The service staff is friendly, efficient and polite. The owners Jean and Michel are two of the nicest people and they respect the tradition of cutting a smoked meat brisket by hand.

*****

The first week of August Joe left to join his family in Alberta, leaving behind a trail of broken hearts. Joe still had three months remaining on the St. Marc street apartment.

He gave me the keys to the apartment and told me use it to its full advantage. I thanked him and told him I would.

I didn't really have the need to use the apartment other than when I needed to do homework or when I finished really late at the Texan, then I would use it to sleep, after all the apartment was paid for until November and it was situated downtown and the apartment was furnished.

And who knows perhaps (because I would be using Joe's apartment) I may become a 'ladies' man just as Joe was.

Probably not but who knows!

cappuccino episode

I had begun to frequent a little coffee shop on rue St. Catherine, between St. Marc and Pierce. *Café St. Catherine* boasted the flashing neon sign in the window; another neon sign blinked 24 hrs.

"Good!" I remember thinking to myself, a twenty-four hours joint. I was able to come and go as I pleased. I would usually go there to breathe, relax, and collect my thoughts after a hard day. What about the coffee you are wondering? It wasn't bad! Not bad at all, if you were lucky enough to receive a fresh cup.

One mid-August Thursday evening, perhaps 10pm, I was sitting on a wobbly wooden chair, seated at a round woodened table. I had just ordered a French vanilla cappuccino, and with me I had brought a book, to help me unwind, and to keep me company while I relaxed and drank my coffee.

While a live band played music in the background, *Café St. Catherine* was about half full with a clientele of all ages, satisfying their coffee fix, munching down 'finger-foods', and pretty much enjoying themselves with various ongoing conversations (and to be heard from some tables…shouting!).

I was just about to begin the book *Moonwebs: Journey into the Mind of a Cult* (1980) by Montreal newspaper columnist Josh Freed when the table (that I was seated at) awakened itself from a long slumber, and kind of wobbled back and forth. My French vanilla cappuccino had also awakened from its sleep and began to spill itself over the table top, dripping down to the black and white tiled floor by way of my pant leg!

Startled, I pushed myself (and the wooden chair I was sitting on) back. I looked around (and as I did), I could feel my left thigh and leg burning. Before my very eyes, (seemingly in slow motion) my French vanilla cappuccino transformed itself into a liquid table cloth. Oozing across and dripping down from the woodened table, on to the left leg side of the blue jeans I was wearing. Trying to rationalize (what was happening) and not quite fully understanding, I quickly lifted myself from the chair, grabbing and using napkins to absorb the French vanilla cappuccino burning my leg.

Patting down and rubbing my wet jeans pant leg, suddenly I heard a voice "Oh I'm so sorry! Here let me help you…"

A second pair of hands with more napkins, dabbing at my French vanilla cappuccino soaked jeans. "I'm supposed to be meeting friends!" a young woman's voice said rubbing me gently, "I accidently bumped into your table!"

"Now I understand!" I said (thinking to myself) "She bumped into my table, thus tipping over the French vanilla cappuccino, thus causing two degree burns on my left thigh and leg. But wait! There was something I did not understand…"

This second pair of hands weren't rubbing the thigh area of my body! Perhaps not realising, these hands were rubbing the area of my crotch. "I can be so clumsy sometimes… Let me buy you another beverage!"

She seemed sincere enough. Casually I responded "Don't worry about it. It's okay." Her rubbing was becoming increasingly more vigorous, "I insist…it's the least I can do." she said flatly. She had stopped rubbing and began dabbing and poking at my crotch. I was becoming sexually aroused….

"Let me clean this mess..." Another voice! I thought to myself. Who is it now? Oh, the waitress... "Can I get you another one?" she asked, attempting to wipe down the table with an already dirty cloth.

"It's my fault!" the first voice with a slight British accent admitted. As for me, I couldn't focus.

"You had a cappuccino...right?" The waitress asked. I turned to her and muttered "Uh huh..."

This twenty something brunette waitress was relentless with her line of questioning, "Was that a large or a small?" Breathing a little heavier than I was before, my heart was beating faster and the rubbing, dabbing and poking at the crotch area of my jeans had stopped.

I looked towards the first voice; a beautiful full figured woman with milky white skin wearing a blue blouse that was slightly unbuttoned, revealing huge breasts and incredible cleavage. With napkins in her hands she was staring down at my crouch area. My penis was now awake and almost fully erect.

A little impatient, the waitress asked firmly again, "Will that be a large or small?"

I was now face to face with the first voice, the huge breasted woman. She appeared to be smiling in a playful way (I swear I heard her chuckling to herself), and with a final dab to my crotch, she introduced herself as Veronica and handed me the damp napkins. Veronica turned towards (the not amused) waitress and asked "What sizes do you have?!"

Looking me straight in the eye, then glancing back down (towards the crotch area), then making eye contact again and finally looking back towards the (now very impatient, arm-crossed, foot tapping) waitress she affirmed "I think a large..."

The waitress abruptly turned (with dirty French vanilla cappuccino cloth in hand), walked a couple of steps, stopped, turned back towards the full figured woman and myself and asked "Is that all?"

Veronica shrugged her shoulders and replied "Yes, a large should do it!"

It toke the waitress a lifetime (it seemed) to reappear with a fresh French vanilla cappuccino.

Meanwhile I introduced myself to Veronica; we shared some small talk and even exchanged phone numbers, promising to "get together".

We exchanged "Goodbyes" and "Goodnights". I watched her as she searched for and found where her friends were seated.

"What just happened?" I asked to no one in particular.

The waitress arrived with my Cappuccino, just as I was sitting back at my table. I thanked her and gave a quick glance to where Veronica was seated.

Episode Epilog:

For some reason Veronica looked very familiar to me, I knew that I had seen her somewhere but I just could not place where.

Then it occurred to me where I had seen Veronica. She was the cashier that served me at the downtown pharmacy when I purchased the box of condoms.

chapter nineteen

About an hour or so later (after the cappuccino episode) I was heading up St. Marc Street towards the apartment. It had begun to rain lightly and walking briskly about twenty feet ahead of me was a woman.

The woman turned into the apartment building I was headed towards. I quickened my pace and opened the glass entrance doors. The woman had her back to me but it was apparent that she was waiting for the elevator.

As I approached the same elevator she turned and appeared to be startled upon recognizing me. She then smiled a big smile and greeted me with a "Oh hello, what are you doing here?"

"I live here." I said "And you?"

"I live here as well". She replied.

"I'm in #308." I informed her.

"Really, I'm on the tenth floor, this is quite the coincidence, don't you think?

"I guess so." I said. Not really sure what I should say.

"So what do you have a two and a half?"

"Yes, a two and a half."

'So you live alone then."

"That's correct and you? She answered my question with another question.

"Did you enjoy your cappuccino?"

"Yes I did thank you."

"Once again I am so sorry for spilling the coffee all over your pants."

"It's okay, accidents will happen." I said as I suddenly realised that I was looking at her blouse that was slightly exposing some beautiful milky white cleavage.

'This elevator takes forever don't you think?'

"It is quite slow."

"So what are you going to do tonight?

"Nothing much, I just want to talk a shower and go to bed."

"Really…I'm a nighthawk I always go to bed late."

"How come..?" I inquired as the elevator doors opened. We both stepped inside; I pressed the elevator buttons for the third and tenth floors, the doors closed and I could feel the elevator moving upward and then abruptly stop at my floor.

I turned to Veronica and said "This is my floor; I guess I'll see you around." I was exiting the elevator when Veronica said, "Yes, maybe I'll come by for a cup of sugar." as the elevators doors closed.

*****

I had just taken a shower and was drying myself when I heard a knock at my door. I wrapped a towel around my waist and looked through the peephole.

It was Veronica, I opened the door an inch or two and she asked. "Do you mind if I come in?"

"Veronica I wasn't expecting anyone. I'm not really dressed, I just took a shower."

"I need a cup of sugar, can I come in please?" I stayed behind the door as I opened it to allow Veronica enough room to come in. Veronica entered the apartment wearing a huge smile.

"I don't have any sugar, I need to buy some." I said and then continued "What are you smiling at?"

"You...you really did just take a shower."

"Well yeah, that's what I said I was going to do" I replied.

"I'm sorry; I didn't mean to disturb you. Did I?"

This was turning out to be an awkward moment. I decided to break the ice and invited Veronica to the sofa. She sat down. I excused myself by saying that I was going to put a pair of pants on. Veronica lifted herself from the sofa and said "You don't have to. I mean I don't want you to feel uncomfortable in your own place. I'm sorry I shouldn't have come."

I could feel the awkward tension in the air and joked "It's okay, I don't want you to feel uncomfortable, your welcome here, and besides it's not as if I opened the door naked. That would have been embarrassing for both of us." I laughed. She didn't. She was looking at me and quietly said "I would like that very much."

Did I hear correctly?. Veronica moved a little closer towards me.

"What did you say?" I asked as Veronica reached for my hand and brought me towards the sofa and with her other hand released the towel from my waist. I felt the towel drop to the floor.

Veronica and I were standing face to face when she replied "I want you naked." She then began kissing me and maneuvered me down to the sofa, feeling my naked shoulders and chest with her hands.

We were passionately French kissing and I was moving my hands over and inside her blouse, touching her huge breasts when I felt Veronica stroking my now erect penis.

"Oh my, my, my you're so big!" she whispered in my ear. I had just unbuttoned her blouse and was about to unfasten her bra when she suddenly stopped and got off the sofa trying to cover herself with her blouse.

"I'm sorry we shouldn't." she said.

"What's wrong?" I asked wanting her to continue.

"This is a mistake."

"What are you talking about?"

"I should be going I'm sorry." Her blouse was almost fully buttoned and she was almost at the door, I followed then she turned to me and saw that I was close to her.

She approached me and again began French kissing me while feeling my body with her roaming hands. Again I felt Veronica stroking my penis only for her to stop. She kissed me on the lips, excused herself, opened the door and left the apartment.

I stood in place, naked, hot and bothered and confused.

*****

I tried to fall asleep on the sofa but could not because of all the tossing and turning I was doing. I lit a cigarette then heard a knock at the door. I checked the time it was 1 am.

I looked through the peephole, it was Veronica. "What does she want now?" I wondered to myself. Then another knock, I looked through the peephole again and noticed Veronica was wearing a woman's rain coat. "It must be raining." I said to myself and opened the door.

Although I was still naked I invited her in while asking "Is anything wrong? Are you okay?" Veronica did not say a word. She walked toward the sofa that was substituting for my bed.

"Is it still raining outside?" Here let me take your raincoat." I said as I opened the closet door and felt for a coat hanger."

Veronica had already untied the belt of her raincoat and was slowly removing the coat from her body, slowly revealing to me parts of a naked body, an incredible naked body.

Although Veronica was a full figured woman she looked fantastic. She had curves in all the right places. Her milky white skin reminded me of…milk. Suddenly I was thirsty for a large glass of Veronica.

Veronica seductively let her raincoat fall to the floor, revealing an almost completely naked body. The only clothing Veronica wore was knee high socks.

I was mesmerised by Veronica's sexy naked body. I wanted her. She slowly approached me reaching for my penis once again and led me to the sofa.

I was lying on my back and Veronica was on top of me, French kissing me, touching my naked body as I was touching her naked body. I moved my hand slowly down towards her crotch, she silently moaned and I could feel that she was already wet. A few moments later I felt her body tremble.

I felt as if I was in a dream. I must have been dreaming for this to be happening.

Veronica continued to moan and moan, louder and louder. I realised then that I was not in a dream and that I was not dreaming. I knew then that we were going to have one hell of a night of passion, and that I was fully ready to enjoy it.

Reantasy, Montreal Epilog

Veronica left my apartment around 7am, she said she needed to sleep after the 'work out' she just had. I invited her to breakfast but she was too tired.

She kissed me goodbye and said I was not only intense but also an incredible lover. I blushed when I thanked her for the compliment.

I dressed and went to a local fast food restaurant for a big breakfast of three eggs, toast, bacon, ham and sausage. I was so hungry.

I was drinking a cup of coffee replaying the night before in my mind.

Veronica I concluded was all women, a full bodied woman with big firm boobs and nice round buttocks. Wow what a body she has.

I paid my bill and was standing outside the restaurant smoking a cigarette and I couldn't help but think to myself how my life seemed to be changing.

I also realised that in mid-August 1980, the city of Montreal was a lonely place to be. Marie moved to Toronto with her family, my friend Joe left to join his family in Alberta and my sister Ellen was gone as well.

My mother was doing better and seemed to be herself again (even though Ellen had moved to Toronto).

George was still in a relationship and seemed to be happy.

I passed my introductory accounting course and was still undecided with what I should be doing with my future and my life. My teacher suggested that I should continue in the accounting field as I seemed to be a quick learner and understood the basics.

Although the No side had won the 1980 referendum, Montreal was still in a transition period, trying to find its way back from the last couple years of friction, business insecurity and slow economic growth.

Montreal's population seemed to be slowly getting over the hump of the 1980 referendum.

Could social, cultural and business prosperity be far off?

Could the province of Quebec bounce back from the 1980 Referendum?

Could the city of Montreal once again become the international city that it once was?

Only time would tell.

I was feeling good about the choices I made regarding my education and my future.

I applied to the Accounting and Management Technology program at Dawson College, was accepted and would be starting the three year course during the next semester

I had received a letter from Marie the week before. She informed me that she had met someone and that she was happy. I was happy for her.

I was eighteen years old in 1980; I was feeling good about myself and happy with the life experiences I recently encountered (especially the encounter I had the night before) and I was looking forward to new ones.

I was finally coming into my own and enjoying it.

I as an individual just like Montreal as a city was slowing getting back on track and finding my way to where I was supposed to be, where I should be.

I'm looking forward to what the future holds in store for this eighteen year old male living in the city of Montreal.

Until next time…

Printed in the United States
By Bookmasters